"She's there," Anse whispered close to Chris' ear.

"Ah-ha. Let's go get her then," Chris suggested with a winsome smile.

Rebecca knelt over a bag, opening it to take out two coal-roasted hens and some cornmeal bread. She looked up at the sound of a snapping twig. Whirlwind's long, handsome body did not fill her gaze. She saw instead three hard-faced white men moving rapidly toward her.

"Look out!" she cried, looking around to find them both surrounded by a dozen leering gunmen.

Whirlwind dove for his rifle. He clutched at it, rolled and came up. A moment later, the heavy barrel of a seven inch Colt .45 slammed into his forehead. Rebecca bit off a scream and tried to run toward her sixguns. A grinning hulk of a man cut her off.

"What are you doing here?" the White Squaw demanded in English.

"We've come to get you, Missy Rebecca," Anse replied.

They knew her name. Rebecca chilled at the realization.

"Where are you taking me? Why?"

"Man wants to see you real bad," Chris replied. "Down Mexico way. Does the name Roger Styles mean anything to you . . . ?

"Unfortunately, yes," Rebecca replied. "The name means death."

WHITE SQUAW
Zebra's Adult Western Series
by E. J. Hunter

#1: SIOUX WILDFIRE	(1205, $2.50)
#3: VIRGIN TERRITORY	(1314, $2.50)
#4: HOT TEXAS TAIL	(1359, $2.50)
#5: BUCKSKIN BOMBSHELL	(1410, $2.50)
#12: BALL AND CHAIN	(1930, $2.50)
#13: TRACK TRAMP	(1995, $2.50)
#14: RED TOP TRAMP	(2075, $2.50)

#17

WHITE SQUAW

BULLWHIPPED BEAUTY
E.J. HUNTER

ZEBRA BOOKS
KENSINGTON PUBLISHING CORP.

Special acknowledgements to Mark K. Roberts

ZEBRA BOOKS

are published by

Kensington Publishing Corp.
475 Park Avenue South
New York, NY 10016

First printing: September, 1988

Printed in the United States of America

This volume in the adventures of Rebecca Caldwell is dedicated with affection to a talented young actress Brook Benkowski with hopes her career will prosper.

EJH

Chapter 1

"I think I can hear the stream, Whirlwind," Rebecca Caldwell Ridgeway offered.

"Ummm," her young companion replied, not wishing to converse on the trail.

"I've ridden all over this country and never encountered it before," the lovely, raven-haired, blue-eyed girl persisted.

Whirlwind sighed and broke his Sioux stoicism. "That's because you stayed on horse trails. You can see that we're walking in the trace of deer now."

Whirlwind, of the Red Top Lodge Oglala band, could not resist the impulse to give his companion anything she wished. Even if it meant talking when he did not think it proper. He would do so, however reluctantly.

"Where does it come from? More importantly, where does it go?" Rebecca asked, genuinely puzzled.

"You will see soon." Whirlwind shifted the coil of rawhide rope on his shoulder, then dropped from the faint trail through an opening at the side of the trace. He slid down a steep bank to the ankle-deep stream bed, offering a helping hand to Rebecca.

"Spring up there," Whirlwind pointed up the mountain slope through a tunnel of thick vegetation. "Falls down that way, water disappears into a sandy wash at the foot of the mountain."

"Oh, how lovely," the half-breed girl exclaimed as her glance took in the far bank, where a small meadow extended around an ancient oak.

"The People used to camp here often in the old days, before the Elk Dogs came," Whirlwind informed her. "Come on, the top of the falls is just around the bend."

Their conversation, in the Lakota language of the Sioux, blended liquidly with the burble of water, heard more distinctly now as they progressed on foot. Rebecca studied the powerful flow of muscle beneath his coppery skin as Whirlwind tied off the end of his lariat to a scrub oak, then dropped over the brink. She suppressed a slight shudder, then stepped close enough to see over. Instead of the dizzy drop-off she had feared, the water fell only some twenty feet to a large pool it had carved in a huge boulder. The crystal sheet spilled over the edge of its catch basin between wide mossy lips, to repeat the process twice more. This created a series of three stair-stepped bathing pools, eroded into solid granite. The sight took her breath away.

It was as though nature had gone all out to provide the world's most luxuriant bathing hall. Tall trees drooped out from the walls of the ravine to close off much of the blue sky above the tumbling stream. Verdant leaves absorbed and hushed the burble of falling water, and blocked any chilling breeze. At the foot of the series of pools, trees and vines mingled with underbrush to lock the dwindling waters into a narrow tunnel with branches interwoven above. The colorful early spring finery of the varicolored foliage softened an otherwise monotonous green.

"All right, it's your turn, come on down," Whirlwind announced.

Blue eyes flashing, Rebecca's moccasined toes sought purchase on the slippery granite as she backed over the edge and let herself down the rope. Her short buckskin dress rode up and Becky grinned as she imagined her companion enjoying the view.

Whirlwind felt as though his innards had started to melt, and his eyes traced a hint of blue vein up the tawny sleek skin of the inside of her thigh, until it disappeared in the area of the dimly perceived, yet taut swell of her buttocks. The heat in his belly spread into the stiffening of his manhood as he reached upward and placed a steadying hand on that glorious derriere.

"Ummm. You see? Nothing to it," he murmured in her ear.

For a moment she clung to him. Her radiant expression lighted the shaded natural alcove. A tingling, chill mist brushed their faces. Slowly their lips came together. A soft murmur rose from deep in Rebecca's throat. She pressed her body tightly against that of the hard-muscled Oglala warrior. All remembrance of the past whirled away. She felt the rising presence of his manhood and thrilled to it. Her lips parted and her tongue darted into his open mouth. They flirted a while, like duelists, then the embrace ended.

Whirlwind released her and wordlessly began to remove his moccasins, hunting shirt, leggings and breech cloth. "I need a swim," he croaked at last, his voice unsteady with passion.

"So do I," Rebecca agreed, pulling off her beaded dress.

Icy and invigorating, the water welcomed them. Delightedly, like small children, they cavorted about for several minutes. Sensing a spreading numbness, which would deaden sensitivity, Rebecca suggested they get out and dry themselves in a patch of sun. Whirlwind readily agreed.

They lay side by side, gazing at a sky so deeply blue that it seemed to go on forever. Their breathing rapidly returned to normal, then roughened when Whirlwind placed a hand firmly on Rebecca's right breast. With thumb and forefinger, he manipulated the large nipple, quickly stimulating it to an erect state. Rebecca began to trace along the muscle-ridged length of Whirlwind's torso, exploring the occasional battle scar and savoring the silken, youthful quality of his skin.

"Before the Moon of Burning Prairie, we should go before the medicine man and announce our joining together," Whirlwind declared.

Any thought of formalizing their relationship sent a chill of caution along Rebecca's spine. She quickly wiped away a forming scowl and rolled onto one side, the better to look at her delightful lover.

"Why, Whirlwind? In all ways but that, we are already man and wife. Everyone knows it and there's no need to . . ."

Whirlwind placed two fingers over her lips, to silence the too-familiar argument. "And besides, you need more time to adjust to your loss and prepare Joey for a new father," he quoted the rest of her argument bitterly from memory. He had used Joey Ridgeway's Oglala name, *Pinzpinzala*.

Deeply sensing his hurt, and anxious not to spoil this moment in this beautiful place, Rebecca took immediate action. She kissed his fingers and pulled his hand away, then wriggled atop him.

"I think . . . you're being . . . stodgy," she teased. "Among the *wasicunpi*, it's fathers with marriageable daughters who want all the proprieties to be observed.

10

I'll bet that you can't keep on being stodgy for long like this."

The rigid pressure of his rising organ quickly proved her point. With the ease of familiarity, she swiftly warmed to the occasion. Her body vibrated with the intensity of her ardor and she grew ready to receive him. Straddling his supine frame, she set to work in earnest to banish his fixation on a Sioux wedding. While her nimble fingers sought out the sensitive spots on Whirlwind's body to tickle him, her hips thrust in a determined rhythm. Delightfully she slid the moist outer portals of her treasure trove against the thick bulk of his engorged lance.

"There . . . there . . . you see? Oh, you're ready now. Oh, yes."

A gasp escaped Whirlwind's full, sensuous lips. He drove upward to meet her. Rebecca cried out and responded energetically. Their surroundings appeared to whirl and fade away.

"Look! Look! Watch us where we become one," she commanded.

"I can't," Whirlwind grunted. "I dare not. If I do, I will expel my seed all too soon and spoil it for us both."

"Only young boys are quick on the trigger," Rebecca taunted. "Take command. Watch us blend together and lose yourself in it. Then tell me who needs the muttered words of the *pezuta-wicása* to find happiness?"

Deprived of the strength to argue, let alone the will, Whirlwind surrendered to the infinite joys of his beloved. When at last their desires had been sated, Whirlwind rested on one elbow. His obsidian eyes, in a wide, coppery face, with full lips and hawk nose, showing only a single pinkish scar from a close encounter with a Crow arrow, combined to keep him handsome. His vigor kept a youthful glow to his skin. Oak leaves and pine needles made a dappled pattern on his chest and belly. A soft, gentle smile curved the corners of his mouth.

"Now I'll show you the secret of the Grandfathers. I heard of it as a boy, but no one in our band knew of its location."

"What is it, Whirlwind?" Rebecca inquired.

"Wait. I'll get it for you."

So saying, he rose and poised on the edge of the pool. With the exuberance of a small boy Whirlwind dove deeply. He remained down a seemingly long time, then surfaced in a shower of droplets. In his cupped hands he held a thick gob of black sand. Rebecca leaned close, unsure as to what made this blob of sediment so important. Then she saw it, glinting in the shafts of sunlight.

Tiny pinpoints of bright yellow. Two, she noted, the size of the nail on her little finger. Softly glowing nuggets of gold!

Crisp and shrill, the notes of the bugle shivered the early morning quiet of the high desert, fifty miles north of San Luis Potosi, on Mexico's central plateau. From far above a golden eagle screed answer. Then it banked away for more peaceful hunting grounds as tiny figures spilled from tents and jumped into prepared rifle pits and the revetments of cannon. From recent experience the majestic bird knew that these sounds and activities on the part of the invader presaged unbearable noise and violence. The white flag fluttering over the encampment meant nothing to him.

Cresting another low swell, some three thousand yards from the encampment, the cause of this turmoil sat on a gaunt, once-proud, white stallion. From his

12

vantage point at the head of a ragged, heavily-armed, column of weary men, he looked back at his charges contemplatively. It required no trained observer to note the bloody bandages and near empty state of their bandoliers, nor the look of weary resignation and hunger on normally fierce visages. Pablo Ordaz raised his arm and halted the column before the rest of its vanguard crested the ridge.

"Ernesto," he ordered his *jéfe* in the gruff, coarse tones of a peon. "Take the men that are in the best shape and have them dig rifle pits along the slope facing the Federales. The rest of the men may set up camp."

"Sí el Comandante," Ernesto Guevera, El Tiburón, replied. "Shall I also collect enough ammunition to fill their bandoliers?"

El Comandante, one-time colonel of Rurales in the neighboring state of Zacatecas, and full-time bandit, nodded, appreciation bright in his obsidian eyes. "By all means. Clean them up and feed them, and pray God they are not required to fire the little we have."

Ernesto handed the staff with its soiled white rag to the heavy-set sergeant beside him and spurred back down the column, shouting orders. A feeble cheer went up. Enraged when he considered the effect on the government troops, Ordaz whirled his white charger and spurred it against the bit, causing the animal to rear.

"Scream you lousy whore's sons! Make them hear it." *El Comandante* hauled out an ivory-handled Obregon and leveled the cocked .45 revolver at the first rank of his men. "Cheer for your lives, *cabrónes,* or die with a Lancer's pike in your guts."

Satisfied that the bellowing of his troops would reach the ears of the Federal soldiers some three thousand

13

yards distant, Ordaz spurred down the backside of the ridge. Catching sight of a detail with shovels moving up, he fired at their heels.

"Run, you sons of she goats. They'll be watching you through field glasses. Make that dirt fly or by all that's holy, I'll shoot you myself. Do you think the Federales will talk peace if they believe you curs are beaten already? Fools! Your heads will decorate their lances for all the pretty senoritas to spit upon, when they ride into San Luis."

"Rider coming, *Comandante*," the portly sergeant bellowed. "A Yaqui scout with a white flag."

"*¡Que bueno!*" Ordaz exclaimed under his breath. "So they will talk after all. Ernesto!" *El Comandante* bellowed. "Get those men up here, and hide the wounded in the barrancas. Keep everyone busy, and away from the messenger, except my personal guards. Get that tent up, you sons of slavering cur bitches."

Rudolfo Nerva jumped to obey his superior's commands. Five minutes later, heart still pounding, Ordaz eased into a camp chair at a shaky card table and slid documents, pen and ink from a cardboard book file. He spread them before him, took the lid from the ink bottle, then uttered a sharp curse. With apparent ire he turned the papers right side up. On the crest of the hill, Ernesto also cursed.

Then he ran for his horse, El Dracón. Spurring down the hill toward the defense perimeter, El Tiburón headed for the Yaqui messenger who had been joined by three of his own Yaqui scouts. El Tiburón shouted to them in an attempt to forestall conversation before his arrival. He knew they were apt to mention the deplorable state of his troops and supplies, yet he dare not offend these dangerous savages. El Tiburón cursed himself for not having foreseen this. His troops were

14

too terrified of the Yaquis to interfere with them and the Indians did not speak enough Spanish for one to be sure they had understood their orders. Damn situations where a man must hire from the same tribe as his enemy. He neared the group and reined in with a spray of caliche.

After the formalities, the messenger made known his errand. "There is a gully midway between our two camps. *El Coronel* desires to hold the peace conference there."

"Agreed," El Tiburón said tightly. He wondered what else the Federale colonel might want.

"May I make a mirror signal to our camp, so that a detail can go out and erect a sunshade there for the peace conference?"

"Yes, of course. Go right ahead," El Tiburón responded, indifferent to the sarcasm in his voice. How was it that this Yaqui *cabrón* could speak such excellent Spanish?

"Then this meeting is concluded," the messenger announced. "I will join you on the trail to your camp."

Anger flared at this summary dismissal by an underling. El Tiburón all but shot the emissary of the Federales. Then he thought better of it, turned El Dracón's head and trotted off. Exercising careful diplomacy, he convinced his scouts that this was not the time nor place for an old home week conclave. Out of earshot, he instructed his chubby sergeant.

"*Sergento,* see to it that the Federales detail is counted on the way out and make sure the same number of men return after the shelter is built."

"*Seguro, Jéfe,*" the moon-faced non-com responded with a careless salute.

His message sent, the emissary cantered up to El Tiburón. He remained silent all the way to where *El*

Comandante waited him. Ordaz rose from his rickety chair to greet the messenger and offered him wine and refreshments before opening their talk. Not alone did El Tiburón's guards wonder where such luxury had come from. The messenger found it difficult to believe all of this rag-tag army was so well provisioned, particularly since his cousin Coyóte had greeted him with the news that they were on the verge of starvation. He drank deeply, not liking the sour bite of the dry beverage. He much preferred *pulque,* or mescal. At last the talk turned to the business at hand.

"It is the desire of *El Coronel* that not more than three commissioners are sent from your camp. His own party will consist of four men, one a noncombatant."

"I see no reason that we should not also have four representatives," Ordaz countered, while his well-armed, hastily cleaned up troops strutted around the conference table.

"It is the wish of *El Coronel,*" the messenger answered simply.

Ordaz considered his real condition to the sham he manifested for benefit of the enemy. "Well . . . if that is what is truly needed, I'll not make an issue of it at this time. We will be ready in two hours' time. Now, come, eat some more and drink to your content. There is plenty for everyone."

If only that were so, Ordaz thought darkly, he would smash these *hijos de sus madres* into a red paste. More than a dozen times so far he had crushed the best the government in Mexico had sent after him. Only now . . . now.

16

Chapter 2

In the shocked silence, a variety of bird song came from the trees above. Squirrels chided the invasion by the two-legged beings. Rebecca reached out a tentative finger and stirred the thick mud in Whirlwind's hands.

"Gold," she whispered at last. "Is this . . . all of it?"

"Oh, no," Whirlwind answered casually. "Come on down with me and see."

Without effort, he reversed his position and made a surface dive. Rebecca followed immediately after. It took little time for the swiftly moving water to clear the murky deposit Whirlwind had released from his hands. With their chests nearly scraping the hard packed, heavy sand on the bottom, Whirlwind began to point out the features of this hidden treasure. Using careful, precise movement, Rebecca unraveled the mystery.

Black sand some five inches thick, and flecked with small nuggets, covered the bottom. Below that, tiny flakes of gold dust, some large as a steel nib for an ink pen, so densely packed that Becky had trouble driving her fingers into it, lay in an inch thick layer. Excitement caught at Rebecca, yet the strain of their lungs forced the young couple to surface for air. Gasping, Rebecca shook and wiped the water from her face.

"It's fantastic. I want to look further."

"Go ahead, *Sinaskawin*," Whirlwind offered. "I'll dive with you."

Breath restored, they dove once more. She squirmed through the water, following a straight line to one edge of the pool, then part way around before coming up for air. On the third dive, she completed three quarters of the circular basin. In varying amounts, she found gold everywhere. With a powerful upward thrust they surfaced.

"The other pools?" she asked, amazed, yet eager.

"Are like this."

"It's . . . too much to take in," Rebecca gasped. "All that wealth. Let's get out before we chill too much to dive."

On the bank she attempted to make a rough estimate of the extent of the glory holes. It must be in the tens, no maybe the hundreds of thousands, she gauged. And there could be more.

"This has to have come from somewhere," Rebecca began to frame her thoughts aloud.

"Yes. Sun Boy dropped it here," Whirlwind answered simply.

"I, ah, think it more likely that it washed here from upstream. With Sun Boy's help, of course," she hastened to add. "Let's trace it down, see if there's any chance of someone coming on the source from above."

They dressed quickly and scrambled up the rope, then started off along the watercourse. Rough going at first, the steep bank gave way to a meandering stream that led up a gradual slope and through vegetation so thick they had to stoop in places. Along the way, Rebecca noted that the streambed contained a few streaks and sworls of the black sand, but no trace of the shiny metal did she find.

Then she and Whirlwind reached a low fault of quartz that looked as though it might have created a tiny waterfall, before the relentless water wore it down to the level of the streambed. Traces of various strata shimmered in the sunlight, from chalky white to an odd dull gray, with a layer of pinkish crystals near the bottom.

"Let's get out of our clothes and check the creek," Rebecca suggested.

"What for?" Whirlwind inquired. "Are you feeling . . . ?" he let the randy suggestion hang.

Rebecca turned on an impish smile. "Perhaps. If you ask in a nice way, and later, after we make sure."

"Sure of what?" Whirlwind repeated, uncomprehendingly.

"I want to be positive that there is no trace of the gold around here to give away your secret," she answered.

In no time they splashed in the cool water, which curved around the base of the ridge, cutting away at its surface. After long and careful examination, Rebecca satisfied herself that no wandering stranger could discover the presence of gold by checking this stream. All the while she argued with herself about the best course to take.

Too readily she could visualize what the whites would do to this peaceful meadow and Whirlwind's little paradise if they got wind of the treasure. Yet, could she in clear conscience allow the Red Top Lodge band to exploit this find? Material wealth in abundance would ruin the way of life for the Oglala, create jealousies and contention. Worst of all, there was enough of a fortune there to turn every last one into a shiftless alcoholic, but not enough to keep them insensible for the rest of their lives. What to do?

Buy land for them? Not a chance. Indians, even those counted and on the reservations, were not citizens. Their titles to the land would not be recognized. The source of their money would be challenged, which would lead to discovery of the gold and a rush would start. Which would effectively displace them again, since the pools lay on the Rosebud Agency. Unresolved, her problems continued to plague her.

Collapsing his old brass telescope with an audible snap, young Lieutenant Xavier Ernesto Alvarado Polanski returned it to its case. With an annoyed shake of his head, he turned to survey his company of mounted Lancers at the foot of the hill. Xavier didn't like any part of the current operation. Pablo Ordaz was nothing but a bloody-handed bandit who claimed an offhand connection to Ochóa and Carvalles, simply more bandits who aspired to a revolutionary image. If that were not so, would his commander have placed him here, out of sight of the bandits, but able to observe them? But then, there was the *gringo*.

Señor Roger Styles, a *norteño*. He brought papers purported to be directly from Diáz in *la Capital*. What business did he have sticking his nose into our internal affairs? It was said he was a really big *ladrón*, a bandit and thief of imperial proportions in the United States of the North. Now he had the favor of Don Porfiro Diáz, or so it seemed. A negotiator? Did the great Juarez need a negotiator to deal with the French?

"¡Esta señor me cae gordo in el culo!" Xavier was unaware he had spoken aloud until his sergeant questioned him.

20

"¿Que, teniente?"

"Wha— Oh, nothing, Sergeant Alvarez. I was thinking of the fancy *gringo.*"

Alvarez smiled broadly. His narrow, Indian face beamed with good humor. "He gives me a pain in the ass, too, *teniente.*"

Polanski touched him lightly on one shoulder. "Then we are together in that, eh?"

The young Lancer officer lapsed into silence again. He was not at all happy about the *gringo,* nor what he knew of his *comandante's* orders. These bandits were at the end of their rope. Xavier had heard the Yaqui scout's report, one in considerable detail. In their current weakened state, the rabble should be annihilated right here and to hell with the politicians in *Ciudad Mejico.* Too late for that now, he concluded, as he watched Pablo Ordaz and his deputation swing into saddles and set out for the sunshade where the conference would be held.

"Comandante, they are on the move," Xavier called out to his superior, then cantered into place at the headquarters tent, to join the party. That left his senior NCO in command of the Lancers, Xavier reflected, yet no worry. With Alvarez there, nothing would go wrong.

A mountain grouse clucked scoldingly as the mounted bandits trotted out of camp, resplendent as possible in their once gaudy uniforms. With smoldering eyes, El Tiburón watched. He had been left behind, in command of the encampment while Ordaz, the hefty sergeant and Hector Blancos headed for the peace talks.

"*¡No te dejes poner los ojos verdes!*" he called out.

"Don't worry," Ordaz joked back. "There's not a sheep big enough to put wool over these eyes."

Mierde! El Tiburón thought angrily. He still considers this as a joke. In all of Ernesto's years of study, in all the dangerous meetings in the dark of night, he had developed a deep appreciation of the absolute importance of each element that spelled political success. Ordaz had appeared a prime candidate to put forward. Amiable, pliable, not too bright. As long, the angry reflections continued, as he took orders. Ernesto Guevera accepted the fact he had been compelled to work through Pablo Ordaz, because of his total lack of empathy with men. Particularly the *peon* class. A self-proclaimed champion of the down-trodden and the poor, university educated Ernesto Guevara held his less fortunate fellows in abject contempt. He was feared, but not respected. Able to connive, but not to lead. A planner, but not an executor.

An intellectual, oh, yes, that he was. He had taken the shark for his *nom de guerre,* since he knew it perfectly fitted the men's image of him. With cold calculation, he deliberately chose to enhance the terror and revulsion as a tool of manipulation. As a student in Europe, he early became a disciple of Marx and Engels, wisely discarding their utopian clap-trap, while memorizing the jargon. For even then, Ernesto saw their foolish, impractical writings not as a social system, but as a road to power. Personal power for Ernesto Guervera, El Tiburón, for he scoffed at real social reform. Soon, he knew, the time would come.

A covey of quail burst from the tall grass, spraying

out ahead of the churning legs of the horses. Heavy with gold, Rebecca's beaded Oglala purse weighed on her mind as she and Whirlwind rode back to her lodge on the Rosebud Agency. Where and how could she convert it?

"Whirlwind, this gold could be a problem for the People," she remarked as they slowed their horses to a walk.

"How is that? It's only the white man's yellow metal."

"That's just it," Rebecca continued. "The size and number, to say nothing of the smooth, rounded shape, of these nuggets would shout out that they came from a glory hole, even to the most ignorant of whites. They'd take one look and know this collection had to have been skimmed from the top of a vast treasure. I seriously doubt that any white, or for that matter, any 'civilized' Indian could be trusted with this kind of knowledge."

"You make our good medicine sound bad," Whirlwind declared in a voice verging on a pout.

"Even if we worked carefully and took out only the fine dust from the last pool, Black Hills mining is slacking off enough to cause some excitement over any new find. I want to see this be of benefit to our band. We can buy iron pots, knives, good, warm blankets, canvas that doesn't leak or have holes, and cartridges. Even new rifles. Some of those Remington forty-five-nineties for hunting."

A smile brightened Whirlwind's face. "Better it is Model Seventy-sixes. With Winchesters the soldiers will not be so quick to insult us."

"The treaty agreement won't let you have repeating rifles," Rebeccca came back with direct logic. "That would only cause trouble."

"We are a free people," Whirlwind stated, one fist

23

pounding his chest. "With what the yellow metal will buy, we will have what we want."

"To the whites you are a conquered people. The men who build Winchester rifles, as well as the ammunition for them, would give them to the army also, before they would allow the Sioux to win their freedom and recover their lands. The Remingtons I mentioned will shoot further and straighter than the army Springfields. They will even load a little faster and far more reliably. That alone will cause the army to worry. In short, it is a fine weapon for hunting. Yet, it would not inspire a brave to start trouble he could not finish, and would not give sufficient reason to the Agency police or the soldiers to take them away."

Whirlwind scowled. "If the yellow metal belongs to our band, then the warriors of the band should say what kind of rifles they will have. This should be done in council, or by asking each man his preference."

"That is reasonable enough," Rebecca conceded. "Except for one consideration. Firearms must last a long time, through all sorts of weather. If one breaks, it isn't always easy to obtain repair parts. If each man has his own chosen type and caliber, sharing ammunition is impossible. In times of shortage or want, it could cripple the entire band. This is the way the army functions and they do it rather well, you'll have to admit."

"We are not soldiers," Whirlwind growled. "Free men choose for themselves. We do not walk like a line of ducks into war. We ride and strike for our personal glory. That is the free way."

Before she realized it, her verbalizing of her concerns became a heated debate. In no time they argued passionately. At last, Rebecca sensed Whirlwind wearing down.

"Promise me this. Say nothing to the others until the question of what kind of weapons to buy is settled between us. After all, we still haven't figured out a way to spend the gold."

"Ummmm. It will be as you say."

Coronel Carlos de Nuñoz Escobar, accompanied by Lt. Xavier Alvardo, and the *Sergento Mayór*, along with Roger Styles, approached the shaded council table in perfect time with Pedro Ordaz and his delegation. Voluble, and utterly insincere, greetings followed after the two groups dismounted. The Federales commandant clapped his hands and Sgt. Major Viálobos opened a large hamper that sat beside the table.

"I have arranged for *entremés* and a cooling drink. Will you indulge, *Coronel* Ordaz?"

"*Gracias, Coronel* Escobar. I, too, have brought along some minor refreshments from our camp's surplus. Sergeant Mendoza, bring the basket from your horse, if you please."

"Your generosity is appreciated, Coronel. It is good that we can meet as gentlemen after all this time."

First came glasses of snow-chilled wine from the Federales' hamper. Then sausages and pickled quail eggs from the bandits' larder. Sgt. Mendoza produced a bottle of tequíla. Salt and lime, and a bottle of *Sangrita de la Viuda* completed the table setting. The amenities out of the way, talk of terms began. By the tenor of Ordaz's delivery, it was he who offered terms to the Federales. Escobar listened politely, with an ill-concealed smirk on his lips. At last, he presented his version of their common purpose.

"We have taken most of the territory your, ah, army has wrested from *Presidente* Diáz. It stands to reason, then, that we should be combining our forces under *my* command, no? We are not supplicants, coming to your table, rather victors, dispensing mercy."

Ordaz flushed, his Indian face darkening. "Your guest? We meet as equals."

"*¿De veras?* How is that so?" Escobar returned coldly, then he played his hole card. Based on the information gained by the Yaqui scout, his points became telling. "You are all but beaten. Your men have little food, less ammunition. Their uniforms are in tatters, except for a few strutting popinjays put on display for my envoy. My *Lanceros* could ride over you in half an hour. It is possible we will reinforce your tattered army of band — Ah, but I forget myself. Forgive me, *Coronel* Ordaz," he stated nastily and pointed to Roger Styles.

"This is the personal envoy of *Presidente* Diáz. *Coronel* Ordaz, may I present *Señor* Roger Styles, representing the Federal Government of Mexico. *Señor* Styles, *Coronel* Pablo Ordaz. It is he, *Coronel,* with whom you should deal. *Señor* Styles has generously offered to extend the protection of *Presidente* Diáz to you, as he is authorized to do."

Pablo Ordaz's eyes became obsidian daggers, primed to rip at the head of the *gringo cabrón,* Roger Styles. "We are acquainted, *Coronel* Escobar," Pablo grated out. "I know this *pendejo cobarde gringo* only too well. I helped drag him out of a burning building in Yanqui California, wounded and weak. He stayed with the original *El Comandante* while he recovered. Many of his suggestions made us most powerful in Sonora, as I am sure you know also. Oh, yes, he served us well . . . until — like the faithless bastard he is — he found a new master to serve. Then he betrayed my childhood friend and leader, *El Comandante* to Porferio Diáz and went to serve the politicians in *Ciudad Mejico.* I would rather deal with a desert rattler than this Yanqui snake."

Apparently unruffled by this outburst, Coronel Escobar raised a mediating hand. "A word of caution, *Coronel* Ordaz. Should you fail to agree to the very liberal terms *Señor* Styles has come to offer you, I, *Coronel* Carlos San Antonio Maria Escobar de Nuñez, guarantee that there shall be no quarter. My drums will roll within the hour and the trumpets play *el Déguello* . . . and the dogs will feast on your corpses come nightfall."

Roger Styles cleared his throat, took a bite from a dainty finger sandwich off a silver tray, and spoke softly, in a persuasive tone. "On the other hand, *Coronel* Ordaz, you can walk away from here today, if not a victor, at least under your own power. Your troops will be recognized as the Federales force for the states of Nayarit and Guanajauto. Yourself will receive a probationary commission confirming your rank of *Coronel,* along with commissions for such of your staff as you shall choose from among your fellows. However, *Presidente* Diáz insists that you make a gesture of good faith." Roger shrugged, turned up one palm. "It is nothing, really. A mere token. On behalf of Don Porferio Diáz, president of Mexico, I want the head of the political agitator and enemy of all Mexico, Ernesto Guevera, also known as El Tiburón."

Despite his best effort, *El Comandante* paled with shock. *¡El Tiburón!* His own loyal Shark? "Impossible!" he blurted.

"*Nothing* is impossible, *Coronel,*" Roger returned icily. "Why, we are like brothers. Whatever would the men

27

think of me if I turned on a friend and companion?"

"Perhaps," Roger suggested, "they would praise their leader if he exposed a traitor in their midst. Say a traitor who had been feeding the government with information on your activities and whereabouts?"

"El Tiburón has done this thing?" Ordaz demanded, his wrath rising.

"No," Roger answered levelly. "Yet, that matters little. What counts is that I, and through me, *Presidente* Díaz, will settle for no other token of your sincerity."

"Wh-why is El Tiburón so important?" Ordaz's frantic gaze rested on his two staffers, whose heads seemed to grow lighter as they correctly read their leader's thoughts.

"Simply because Tiburón has been so close to you in the past," Roger explained. "His head is a token, as I have said before. A proof of good faith if you will."

Besides, he sees the same ways to power that I do, Roger thought, though failed to enunciate. It was always better, Roger believed, to eliminate competition before it became strong enough to resist. In the case of the Shark, Roger held all the trumps. The man who understood, and properly employed the theories of Marx would some day be dictator of Mexico. Unfortunately, for himself, Ernesto Guevera failed to properly appreciate the subtle cruelties inherent in Marxian philosophy. Better he be crushed now, to make way for one who did. Roger Styles had not been alone in reflecting on what had been said and what lay behind it.

Lt. Xavier Alvarado was appalled at this callous proposal. He took the few silent moments to rally his scattered impressions. *"Mí Coronel,"* he began an impassioned appeal. "This is outrageous. No civilized nation in the world would countenance such a proposal. No

28

intelligent man would be deceived by it. I am not overly concerned about the treachery being suborned . . ."

"*¡Silencio!*" Escobar thundered. "*Por favór,* Lieutenant, you forget yourself. It is at the request of our ultimate commander, *el Presidente.* Who are we to question him?"

Someone had better, Xavier thought in silent bitterness. No, it wasn't the treachery, his ruminations went on. That was an unexcisable portion of the Mexican nature. It harkened back to the awful punishments and cruel betrayals of their Indian ancestors. It sickened him, but he had learned to live with it. Perhaps it was through the blood of his Mexican father that he managed to take it with little protest. Only, how could *Coronel* Escobar not see through this ploy? The ones to suffer will be the Federales and the Army of Mexico. When Ordaz submits, he will be a tool of this conniving *gringo,* and not a loyal officer of Mexico. Nothing but grief can come of that. With a mental wrench, Xavier forced his attention back to the conversation.

". . . st have time to think over this proposition. What you ask," Ordaz forced out, "is most difficult, and painfully personal."

"You have until sundown," Roger dictated coldly.

Without further remark, Ordaz and his companions rose. "Very well. *Adiós.*"

"*Vaya con diós, Coronel,*" Escobar responded softly.

Wordless in his fury, Lt. Alvarado watched the bandits ride back to their camp. Col. Escobar turned to Roger Styles. "Do you really think that *bandido* will make a good officer?"

"When pigs learn to fly," Roger snapped back, adamant, yet determined to hide his exultation. "Ordaz is nothing. A buffoon. El Tiburón has always been the brains and strategist for the outlaws. An educated man, he has nevertheless dedicated his life to the acquisition of personal power. Although Guevera espouses the philosophy of Karl Marx, he, like anyone of real intelligence, knows it is a subterfuge that is totally unworkable. To put it simply, it is a roadway to power, nothing more or less. It never solves the social ills it purports to address, it is never benign, and it is no more original with the Englishman, Marx, than any of his other babblings."

"Hummm. How is this, *Señor* Styles?" Escobar inquired, hooked on an opportunity to have a good discussion.

"Nearly two thousand years ago, in ancient Rome, there lived a man of minor noble rank, named Catalinus. He was a contemporary of Julius Caesar, Cicero and the dictator, Sulla. Like many men of his rank, he found himself involved in several conspiracies, with political power as the ultimate prize. Catalinus formed one of his own. It's come down to us as the Cataline Conspiracy," Roger added parenthetically. "In it he fashioned himself as champion of the masses. He exhorted the lowly workers and the classless unemployed to rise up and tear down the temples of wealth, the, ah, homes of his fellow equestrians, by the way. By so doing, he offered them the panacea to cure all their financial and social ills. He spoke to them often and faithfully had a scribe set down all he said. In one speech, when he sought to raise up the working class to sack Rome, he promised a new government to be created out of it, one which would redistribute the wealth, tax the rich and give to the poor, all would work, each according to his ability, and all would share, each according to his needs. In conclusion, he urged them on with a stirring slogan." Roger paused in his narrative and studied the faces of his entranced audience.

"Perhaps you are not familiar with Professor Marx's little red leather-bound volume, gentlemen. But if you were, you'd know that every one of those promises is listed as an article of faith in his Manifesto, right down to the final exhortation, which Catalinus rendered as, 'Workers of Rome, unite! You have nothing to lose but your chains.' And none of us, I'm sure, want a monster like El Tiburón running amuck in Mexico quoting this drivel."

"¡Por diós! I underrated the astuteness of our Presidente," Escobar blurted out.

And you still underrate mine, Roger smirked. He let his delight explode into a chuckle as he pointed at the retreating bandits. "Look. Those two have every intention of seeing El Tiburón's throat cut, rather than their own. See how they gesture to emphasize whatever they're saying? Even now they are justifying the action to their chief. It may be brutal, it may be, as you say, Lieutenant, uncivilized. But it is effective."

Chapter 3

Curls of smoke rose from outdoor cooking fires, as dogs yapped and children shrilled their playful way through the circled ranks of lodges. The first pastel bars of a spectacular sunset tinted the western horizon. Now a burnished copper coin, the sun hung three fingers breadth above distant hills. Removed by some eight miles from the main encampment, the village of the Red Top Lodge Oglala appeared still prosperous and peaceful. The camp crier made note of the arrival of Rebecca and Whirlwind, announcing it at the outer hoop and again near the lodge of the chief.

At once, a slightly built, though muscular, youth of thirteen broke off a game of *yugmi oyućayuspapi na, ćankpe un poge nawićazuzu po* and ran to take charge of their horses. Despite his age, and newly acquired status as a young hunter, he wore only the breech cloth and moccasins of a child. His straw-white, braided hair and starkly blue eyes contrasted with the deep bronze color of his skin. Except for these startling differences, Joey Ridgeway could pass for a typical Oglala boy. The violent game had given him a bloody nose, scraped knees and a knot on one elbow. He couldn't be happier.

"Hau-cola, Tatekohomni, ina," Joey greeted in Lakota.

Upset at his still-bleeding injuries, Rebecca blurted out, *"Joey!"* At the fleeting frown on his high, smooth forehead, she corrected herself using the name he preferred. *"Pinzpinzala.* What happened to you?"

Joey—Little Prairie Dog to his adopted Oglala band—grinned hugely. "We were playing the attack-upset-smash-smash-nose, kick-and-swing game. Our side's winning."

Pleased that he had called her "mother" in Lakota, Rebecca produced a mock shudder. "I'd hate to see what the other side looks like."

"Kehala got knocked out," Joey said proudly. Quick to note the adults' frowns of disapproval, Little Prairie Dog darted a hand out to take the bead-decorated, braided horsehair bridles. "I'll rub them down with sweet grass and put them in the herd where the grazing is best."

Rebecca set about gathering more firewood, setting the evening cookfire and assembling the pots, bowls and utensils she would need. Whirlwind entered the lodge silently, his lips formed into an angry pout. At the stream, marked with the sign of her lodge, the claw mark of her father's totem, Iron Claw, she discovered a trio of expertly cleaned rabbits. Joey had been showing off his hunting skill. Abruptly she decided to broil them for supper. The left-over Agency beef stew could wait for breakfast. While she worked, her troubled thoughts continued.

This had been their first major quarrel. She knew her position was the right one. *Tatekohomni*—Whirlwind—was behaving like a spoiled child. No, he was only being what he was; a proud, arrogant, Oglala Sioux warrior. But then, by white standards, Indian children were shamelessly spoiled. Didn't it stand that this laxity would produce . . . She bit off that speculation before it fully formed. Yet . . . his insistence that

33

they speak the sacred words before the medicine man; *mitawiću*—I take this woman for wife—and *mihigna*—my husband—was becoming an obsession. Add his present attitude about the firearms issue and it was nearly more than she could endure. He had come to their lodge long ago now. Surprisingly, Joey had welcomed Whirlwind as an uncle, at least.

They boy couldn't help but know that Whirlwind wanted to make a family of them. At times he hinted he'd like that, also. Years past, when she had no other life, no discernible future, beyond being wife to a young warrior of the Red Top Lodge band of Oglala, the obligations and submission required of being so did not bother her. Now, after years of independence . . . ? Another unanswered question. Joey returned, his face alight with some new adventure, a white grin spreading across his face. He had washed up, she noted, and managed to walk with a certain swagger.

"Wolf Brother says that I am ready for my *ihambleiciyapi*." He pointed proudly to the bulge of his almost omnipresent erection. "He asked me about this and how my seed pods fared. When I told him, he said that I should hunt my herbs and make ready. At the next full moon, I will take my vision quest."

Tears sprang to Rebecca's eyes and she bit her lip to keep from crying out with motherly sounds that would only hurt the child in his pride of growth. Too soon. Oh, Great Spirit, it is too soon for him, her mind appealed. He's only a baby. Not so, her eyes belied her. The physical evidence and his frank, open discussion of his awakening sexuality far from disturbed her. She had lived too many years among the Sioux to be inhibited or scandalized by the bizarre sex taboos of the whites.

From the time that she and her mother had been brought as captives to this band of Oglala, Rebecca

34

had learned to accept nudity, sex-oriented remarks and casual foreplay as every bit as natural as yawning, sneezing, or body elimination. The six years before her escape saw her married, a mother of a healthy boy, her child killed and widowed on the same day. She had even remarried, only to have a second husband fall to the bloody raids of the Crow. Later experiences had modified her outlook, but failed to make her prudish. Her reaction came from deeply rooted maternal instincts toward her stepson that sought to protect him from the ordeal she knew he must now face.

"Y-you're growing up so fast, Jo—*Pinzpinzala*," she managed to force out. "Before long you'll be a warrior. Look," she sought to change the subject. "I'm fixing your rabbits for supper."

If possible, Joey glowed even more. "I . . . hoped you'd like them."

"They're wonderful. And so fat. Whirlwind will relish one all for himself."

"*I'll* eat a whole one, too," Joey declared boastfully. "Then I will go to sleep in the lodge of Uncle Tall Elk. That is . . . if I may," he added, staring at his pigeon-toed moccasin tops, lids masking his cerulean orbs, in proper show of humility and obedience.

Rebecca could refrain no longer. She took the boy in her arms and hugged him. "Yes, go along and do that. Beaver is getting close to his time to become a man. You two will have much to plan."

Sunset had faded to a thin band of orange on the far mountains before Whirlwind came out of the lodge. He stood proudly, then sniffed deeply. "Are those rabbits I smell broiling?"

"Yes, *Pinzpinzala* shot them today," Rebecca answered.

"Good. I'm hungry." He started to walk back inside, then paused. "Will I have the company of my woman and the boy at supper?" he inquired.

Rebecca knew it for the closest to an apology he would ever make. It lightened her heart. Eagerly accepting his best effort at reconciliation, she nodded solemnly. *"Pinzpinzala* informed me he would eat a whole rabbit by himself."

"Ho! He is outgrowing his breech cloth. Tell that rascal that what he doesn't eat, he'll wear around his neck," Whirlwind said jokingly. He breathed stentoriously again. "The sunset is beautiful. And, I am told, there will be a lover's moon tonight."

There was more than a hint of lust in his dark eyes when the last light of the sun faded and he re-entered the tipi. Rebecca looked forward with anticipation to their *real* reconciliation after the light went out in their skin lodge, one of the few left in the village.

"Pasájero que viéne!" a Federale sentry called out in the dusk.

Lt. Xavier Alvarado whipped up his ancient brass telescope and peered intently into the waning light. With effort, he made out the figure of the hefty sergeant who had accompanied Ordaz to their camp. As the rider drew nearer, Xavier discerned the grisly parcel the larded non-com bore in one hand. Think fingers tightly grasped the long, black hair of the wide-eyed head of El Tiburón. The grim trophy clearly portrayed the former bandit's utter surprise at the moment of his untimely demise.

"Nuestro Señor tiener merced," Xavier gulped, making the sign of the cross. "May his soul, and those of all the faithful departed, rest in peace."

"A tender heart, Lieutenant?" Coronel Escobar inquired from the gathering darkness. "For a bandit, such as he?"

"No, sir. For any man whose soul has departed this earth. It is our obligation as Christian gentlemen, *que no?*"

"Sometimes, Alvarado, I think you should have taken Holy Orders," Escobar chided gently.

"*Father* Xavier?" the young officer returned lightly. "Had it been so, the Fates no doubt, would have had me assigned as a military chaplain."

They chuckled softly. Then Escobar sighed heavily. "At least our *gringo, Señor* Styles, has what he wanted. May God defend the right."

"With swine like Styles about, that may be exceedingly difficult," Alvarado observed tightly.

For six days, Rebecca Caldwell Ridgeway mulled over the problem of the new-found fortune. She discarded one plan after another. At last memory stirred a new course in her deliberations. She knew of someone after all who could be trusted with the converting of gold to cash. It would require a trip to Nebraska. There she could appeal to old Orville Styles, a rancher and merchant, and ironically enough, father of her worst enemy. The more she considered it, the better she liked the idea. Surprisingly, when she revealed this turn to Whirlwind, he approved. They laid plans for an immediate departure. Then the Moon of the Burning Prairie (April) waxed toward full.

"It's my time of testing, mother," Joey explained urgently, standing with arms crossed over bare ribs. "Today we go to the sweat lodge to be purified. For three days we will fast and pray there. Then we go forth to find our vision. You cannot go when that's happening, mother. Please."

Rebecca's heart throbbed with mixed sorrow and pride. "Of course I can't," she readily agreed. "How many of you are there?"

"Five, counting *Kehala* and Badger. They're waiting for me now." His voice held a tone of misery at the delay.

"Go with the Great Spirit, then, my son," Rebecca responded as a proper Oglala mother.

Then she reached out and embraced *Pinzpinzala* and bussed him on the forehead. She followed that with a kiss full on the lips.

Joey *liked* being kissed on the lips. But he would rather it was Raven's Wing, or Blue Willow. With them he could safely kiss back and they could fight the battle of the tongue lances. He found himself stiffening rapidly as he concentrated on Blue Willow. She of the small hands and feet, and delicate features, who was *so good* at *ceazin*. He could almost feel her soft, moist lips closing around his rigid *ce*. No! He must not think of such things. He must remain pure for the *inipi*. And, following the sweat-lodge ceremony, the three days and nights of dreaming to find his vision. The everyday, pleasant things of life — food, drink, sex — must be pushed away to make room for the Spirit to show him the way of his future.

For a moment, his thoughts stunned him. How could he think like that? He was Joey Ridgeway, a white boy and a Christian. Yet, somehow, this other way, this Oglala way, seemed so right, so *natural*. And they didn't care if a kid fooled around a little on the path to growing up. Realization of that sent a shiver down Joey's spine and in an instant he became again *Pinzpinzala*, Little Prairie Dog of the Red Top Lodge Oglala. Adjusting his newly found, and only half-formed dignity, he bid his mother a cool farewell and set off to the lodge of the medicine man. A pang in her heart, Rebecca watched him go.

Like the rest of the women whose sons of twelve and

thirteen had gone off on their vision quests, Rebecca endured the ordeal with silent stoicism, and growing trepidation. What if Joey, *no, Pinzpinzala* were to reach out at the wrong time and grasp the brow strap, instead of the bow string? How would he take to being a *heyoka,* a contrary?

Rebecca had no idea of her stepson's orientation. He ran with the boys, swam and played with the boys, spoke mostly about the other boys. Yet all Sioux lads of his age group did that. Could it be that he would actively seek the life of a *winkte?* Her heart ached at the thought. Even so, part of her argued that he was, as the whites said, all boy and a yard wide. He had fought for his rights and property, hunted and killed game, and when necessary, taken the life of a human being. He could never be content with that sort of existence. It mattered not that thousands of mothers before her and thousands more in time to come anguished over the same gnawing insecurity. For Rebecca, it happened for the first time and with such intensity as to blind her to all else.

Particularly so when first one, then a pair, then the fourth youngster returned from his quest, to be welcomed as an adult into the band. Joey did not take his place. Another day and night went by. When at last, Joey came strutting proudly back to the village, alone and naked as he had gone, it took the loud clamor of Rebecca's neighbor women to make this known.

She caught sight of him as he disappeared into old Wolf Brother's lodge, to there whisper secrets into the ear of the aged medicine man. This completed, along with his first ritual smoke, acknowledged outside the lodge with much laughter for the high-pitched coughing it generated, the wrinkled wise man came forth. Beside him stood a suitably dressed, and proudly grinning *Pinzpinzala,* for the naming ceremony.

"Hiyupo!" Wolf Brother called unnecessarily, for fully half the band had gathered. "Come forward," he repeated. "There is a new young man, a brave hunter among the People. His totem is the golden eagle, and his is to be called by those who know him, Sharp Eye. Bring food, and drink, warm the drum, and make him welcome."

Of a sudden, those ritual words took on new meaning for Rebecca. Eyes wet with tears, she hurried forward to acknowledge her son. He looked terrible, all bony, knobby, hollow eyed. She would fix all of his favorites. Feast him until his belly stuck out. Then she caught the eye of Whirlwind. After hugging her beloved boy, she hurried to his side.

"There is much to do," Whirlwind told her sternly. "In three days' time we will leave to visit your white man friend."

"But there's *Pinz—*, ah, Sharp Eye to feed back to strength," Rebecca started to protest.

Whirlwind gave forth a hearty, understanding chuckle. "Pamper him if you must. Then, in three days, leave him with his Uncle Tall Elk, while we make our way south."

"Of course. As you wish," Rebecca replied, with all the humble resignation of a Sioux wife. Even without saying the sacred words, had it somehow happened? she mused in silent confusion.

Chapter 4

Rivulets of sparkling rainwater from a spring thunderstorm ran briskly along the well-tended ditches on either side of the sturdily constructed turnpike. Nebraska, Rebecca Caldwell Ridgeway observed, was rapidly becoming civilized. She and Whirlwind cantered loosely along the high road toward Deer Creek. Not for the first, nor the last, time did she think it ironic to be calling on Orville Styles.

This portly, gray-haired old gentleman had for years been a close friend of her grandfather. He had also been father to Roger Styles, an arch criminal, who had acted as brains behind the Bitter Creek Jake Tulley gang. The elder Styles had disinherited his son upon his discovery of Roger's criminal activities, and aided Rebecca in the opening rounds of her quest for vengeance. Several times, over the following years, she had slipped away to visit his neatly kept, highly prosperous farm.

Orville Styles raised blooded horses, as well as remarkable wheat, hay, and corn. He grew in wealth over the passage of time. He had given her a high-spirited sorrel gelding, Ike, to pursue her search for the outlaws who had traded her life and that of her mother for their freedom from the Sioux. His only condition to unlimited help had been that Rebecca promise him that when she caught up to his wayward son, she not be the one to tell him the details.

That had proven a wise request, for most of the forty men who rode with Bitter Creek Jake Tulley died horrible deaths. That included the leader and, at last, her uncle Ezekial Caldwell. Before his fiery death, Ezekial had murdered Rebecca's husband of four short months, Grover Ridgeway, and her elder stepson, Peter. Grief and a sense of desolation had brought Rebecca back to her father's people, the Red Top Lodge Oglala. Now she drew deliberately closer to the one place which would open old sores and crust them with a new layer of salt.

Not that a man so kindly disposed and upright as Orville Styles would intentionally hurt her. To the contrary, he could be counted upon to always shield her if possible. Yet, as the last half mile dwindled to a short ride up the farm lane, unpleasant memories kept rushing back.

"No, ma'am, I bought the place from Orville six months ago. He's moved into town." The long, sunburned face of the rangy farmer in the doorway radiated sincerity. He brushed at a lock of straying brown hair and nodded in the direction of Deer Creek. "Orville was gettin' up in years, as I'm sure you know. An' that bank of his was prosperin'. So he decided to give up farmin' and settle close to his other interests."

"Bank? I didn't know he had an interest in the bank," Rebecca responded, surprised by this news.

"Ain't an interest. He *owns* the hull thing," the farmer, a man named Jenkins, informed her. "Didn't know Orville had any, ah, breed friends, if you'll, ah, pardon the expression, ma'am."

42

"We've not been here in a long while," Rebecca responded. "Thank you, Mister Jenkins. I suppose we'll be on our way. Banks don't need any horse breakers or fill-in cooks."

Rebecca and Whirlwind had chosen to travel incognito, as a pair of Delaware, or "half-breeds", who as such are not confined to a reservation and worked the outlying farms and ranches, did a bit of trading and guided hunting parties of wealthy Easterners. It would allow them to move freely, yet not be "seen" by nearly everyone. After leaving the farm, they decided to continue the charade. If Orville Styles would help, the disguise would assure their means of exchanging gold and transporting valuable goods to the Rosebud Agency.

"What can I do for you, lady?" a squint-eyed teller asked of the apparent "breed" squaw who stood at his caged window.

"I, ah, have some gold to exchange for hard money," Rebecca Caldwell Ridgeway told him.

She wore a paisley dress, more a tent, she thought of it, with high moccasins and tufts of the same cloth in her braided hair. A soft, black, floppy hat crowned her head. She looked every inch a Delaware woman. For years, the Delaware tribe had explored the prairie and the shining mountains. It became popular to call them "half-breeds" to distinguish these individuals from the hostile tribesmen of the plains. The name stuck long after the fur trade dwindled and the mountain men departed. Brass wristlets and other dangling jewelry completed her disguise. To her it was obvious that the teller bought her as genuine. His pleated forehead and wrinkled nose told it all.

"We buy at nineteen-fifty an ounce, sell at twenty," his disapproving tone informed her.

"That will be quite all right," Rebecca informed him. From her beaded clutch purse she produced a soft deerskin pouch. This she handed to him.

"Scale's back there," he explained as he rose from his stool.

"Surely you wouldn't mind bringing it out front for a lady, would you?" Rebecca prompted in a coy tone.

"Can't do that. Have to rebalance it."

"Then may I come back with you?"

"Well, ah, I suppose. That gate over the end of the counter," he grudgingly allowed.

"Thank you," Rebecca managed primly.

Plaster walls had been painted a bright yellow to the patterned tin ceiling, with a wainscoting of dark wood extending downward from five feet to the hardwood floor. To one side, behind the tellers' cages, a sturdy counter provided space for a scale, weight set and cabinet for reagents to test the purity of gold specimens. The teller led Rebecca there.

Without a word he set to examining her booty. He clucked with surprise several times, then began to hum a gay tune. "This is remarkably pure gold, ah, Miss. The dust and the nuggets. Where'd you say you got this?"

"My man was paid in it. For breaking mules for some miners in the Black Hills," Rebecca lied smoothly.

"Ummm. Musta been holdin' on to it for a while. There's not been any of this quality get down here in a long time. Let me weigh 'er and we'll see what you have coming."

While he worked, a tall, portly man stepped from a corner office. Rebecca immediately recognized Orville Styles. His advanced age hardly told on a pink, beaming face. He looked directly at her, showing no sign of familiarity. Rebecca hesitated. It might be wise to continue the illusion as planned.

"Here we are, Miss. Twenty-two ounces. At nineteen-fifty, that comes to four hundred·twenty-nine dollars. Would you like it in coin or currency."

"Paper is no good in a rainstorm. Coin, please," Rebecca responded, keeping to her role.

Orville Styles crossed the room, through a maze of tables, to a mousey, bald man seated at a rich-looking roll-top desk. Ignoring what went on at the gold counter, he bent low and spoke softly. The clerk produced a scroll-edged piece of paper, which Styles read, pushing his lips in and out as though munching something. He nodded sharply and took the document with him to his private office. Rebecca let out a soft sigh. Accepting the money, she thanked the teller and departed. The plan had worked quite well. Next phase would be some judicious shopping and another visit to the bank.

Orville Styles rose from his desk with a flourishing of hands and a broad smile. "Well, if I had known, I'd have met you at the front door. The Widow Ridgeway was a stranger to me, but you're certainly not. Come, sit by me and tell me everything, Becky."

"Thank you, Mister Styles. There's a lot to cover," Rebecca answered.

Dressed in a new spring outfit she purchased the previous afternoon, Rebecca had presented herself at the bank as the Widow Ridgeway. The teller who had served her before failed entirely to recognize this lovely young woman. But then, he didn't really *see* half-breeds anyway. He had ushered her to Orville's office and

45

knocked for admittance, announcing her as informed. When Rebecca entered, the elder Styles blossomed.

"Come now, in my advanced years, there's no call for formality between us. Call me Orville. You really are the Widow Ridgeway?"

"That's right," Rebecca answered. For the next hour, while they relaxed over coffee and rolls, she outlined to Orville Styles the events since last they had met. Which eventually brought her to the fiction of the gold and its discovery.

"My stepson, Joey, must be related to a fish. He's always off swimming at one place or another on the ranch. On one occasion when I accompanied him, we discovered a glory hole at the bottom end of a ravine. I don't wish to start a gold rush that would ruin the property and devastate our cattle, particularly since all the gold is in one spot. That's why I've come to you as a source to buy what we produce. I know I can trust in your silence."

"Certainly," Orville pledged. Fascinated by the story, he leaned toward her slightly. "Tell me about this place."

Rebecca gave an accurate description of the geological conditions surrounding the actual find, so that Orville would know that such a deposit did exist, and that there was not apt to be another source nearby. With that concluded and details worked out for future purchases of the raw gold, Rebecca bid Orville good-bye and departed.

Her next stop was at a saddler's shop. A tall, robust, smiling Swede listened carefully to her description of what she wished done with her saddle. When she concluded, he rubbed big, red hands together and spoke with enthusiasm.

"*Ja*, sure, I can do that for you, Miss. The saddle skirt leather is easy to work with. Considering the pattern, though, are you certain you want the decorative roll of piping to be plain? No tooling?"

"Please, make it plain. Even though it will be wrapped around this cordage I've selected, I would like the smooth surface to be inside, the unfinished out. Make the roll with kip and shape it, then close it all off along the bottom seam."

"Pie-colly, if that's the way you want it, that's the way I fix it. Only why leave the upper seam unstitched?"

Rebecca gave him an enigmatic smile. "Oh, just say I have my reasons. And I have the money to pay for such difficult work. I'll be most generous in your case, in return for which, you will not discuss the details with anyone."

"You've got my word on that, *ja* sure."

"Fine then. We have a deal."

Long, narrow tails trailing, the yellow breasted warblers wheeled through a sky made much the bluer by altitude. Nearly the dark of space here at seventy-two hundred feet on the Alta Plana of Central Mexico. To the west spread the jagged saw teeth of the *Sierra Madre Occidental,* to the east the wide, verdant plain where huge black bulls lazed away the days until shortly after their fourth birthday. Then they were rounded up, six or eight at a time and shipped far away in strong boxes to the big cities. There they would thrill the crowd for a brief, violent twenty to thirty minutes and give up their lives. The ranches on which they were raised were not mere *ranchos* or *fincas*, not even mighty *estancias*. They were referred to reverently as *ganadérias*, the homes of the mighty fighting bulls, bred from pure blood lines over two thousand years old in Spain. On the *ganadérias*, everything was done for the sake of the bulls.

47

One of the oldest traditions of bull raising was that the powerful males were never to see a man on foot, or a cape, until the hour of their destiny. Courage, it was held, came from the bloodline of the female. Thus it was that females only were tested against the pic and the cape to determine whether they became the mothers of fighting bulls or tacos. Even this tradition, called the *tienta* had its ritual.

Only those carefully chosen by the *ganádero,* his *mayóral,* or *segundo,* were permitted to enter the testing, or *tienta,* ring to try the bravery of the young heifers. Most odious to the *ganáderos,* the bull raisers, were the *guitános,* the gypsies. Not the fabled dark-skinned people of the colorful wagons, but young boys, and teenagers, who roamed the country seeking a chance to display their skill with the *capóte* and *muleta.* They haunted the *tientas,* when held, and did all they could for a few precious moments on the sand. Worse than this, they frequently jumped the fitted rock fences at night and confronted the sacrosanct bulls in the pasture. The penalty for such offenses were generally a severe whipping by the *segundo,* and a quick trip out of the area. One such *guitáno* was called Rafael Bustámante.

Thin to the point of emaciation, young Bustámante had devoted the last three of his fourteen years to following the bulls. Rafael owned only the threadbare shirt on his back, the soft, off-white, knee-length cotton trousers depended from hips that defined a wasp waist, and the worn, scuffed, leather sandals on his uncovered feet. He had an angelic face, with enormous eyes and an infectious smile. His only valuable possession was the heavy, magenta-and-yellow *capóte,* made of raw silk, with a stiff canvas liner.

It had been given to him by the hand of Miguel

Armentas, El Ciclón, the highest ranked *matador* in all of Mexico. Rafael cherished it more than life itself. Yet it served him as a rain cape, bed roll and shelter from the cold. Rafael traveled with a gang of boys ranging from nine years to fifteen, all seeking to be discovered and make their way to the top, like El Ciclón. This day, however, Rafael had given his companions the slip and sneaked out to see for himself what chances there might be at Las Piedras *ganadéria*.

A new owner had taken over, he had learned. A Coronel Pablo Ordaz, a man of much power and influence, it was said. A man with the backing of the *Presidente* of Mexico. There was to be a *tienta* in two days, in honor of the new *Patron*. Surely a man of such prominence might take pity on a small boy with a gigantic wish to become a *matador?* Rafael would look the place over, listen to what the *váqueros* said among themselves, then make his decision. After that he would tell the others. Careful to avoid the many spines of the abundant cactus, Rafael threaded his way along a shallow ravine, beside the rutted road that led to the Las Piedras *tienta* ring.

Four *váqueros* worked industriously with large brushes and buckets of whitewash on the mud-plastered walls of the viewing stand. Behind them came another with small containers of blue, red, yellow and green paints. He made decorative designs against the stark white background. A boy of twelve or so furiously scrubbed dust from the red brick facings. Two ranch hands replaced a 20 x 20 cm post that supported the *barrera*. Another painted the thick boards of this important fence with bright red. Working with a pair of mules, a grizzled old-timer ran a spiketooth harrow over the arena, preparing it for a new layer of sand. With the warm spring sun beating on his bare head, and the fascinating activity progressing orderly in front of him, Rafael became entranced. His innate caution slid away. The old man with the harrow finished and trotted his team out the large *Entrade de Quadrillas* gate. Flies and fat bees buzzed hypnotically, and Rafael's eyes drooped.

"You have come for the *tienta,* eh, *niño?*" an age-crusted voice inquired from behind Rafael.

Startled, he jumped, then turned rapidly. He wished he had a sombrero to whip off his head to show respect. "*Sí, viejo,* if it is permitted."

The gnarled old *váquero* rumbled deep in his throat and produced a compromise smile. "Alas, *joven,* it is not. But I recall quite well what it feels like, this love of the bulls. *De veras,* long ago, when I was younger than you, I, too, was bitten by the same *toro.* For one long summer I ran away from home and followed the *guitános* from *ganadéria* to *ganadéria.* Only once was I able to unfurl my homemade, rather shabby *capóte* and cape a *vácilla.*" The old man chuckled softly with remembrance. "She was a tiny thing, not even as tall as me, and only six months old. Her horns were no bigger than my pecker. Yet to me she was as huge as a locomotive."

Caught up in the recollection, Rafael asked excitedly, "What happened?"

"Oh, I got knocked over, rolled around in the dirt some. My nose was bloodied. Later that week, my father found me, outside the *Plaza de Toros* in Zacatecas. He took me home. I had a sore butt for a while and the next spring, my father apprenticed me to Curo Martin, who was then *mayoral* here at Las Piedras. I have been here ever since."

"And you are the *mayoral?*" Rafael inquired sincerely. Twinkling eyes and a soft laugh answered him. "Me?

50

Oh, no, nothing so grand for Eloy Herrada. For me, the irony she is complete. I am in charge of the little *vácillas.*"

"Oh, I had hoped . . ." Rafael replied, eyes downcast, one big toe scuffing the dirt.

"That is not to say I am without influence," Eloy Herrado said through a grin. "The rules *are* the rules. But . . . there might be room at the *tienta* to squeeze in one small boy."

Rafael nearly squealed with delight. He did jump up and down, so that Eloy had to reach out and restrain the lad before he attracted unwanted attention. He patted the boy on one rosy, silken cheek. Age has its privileges and the old *váquero* knew how and when best to employ them.

"That is provided you leave here at once. Do nothing to attract attention to yourself, and absolutely *keep away from the bulls.* If you do anything wrong, I won't be able to help you. I won't even know you and this conversation never happened. *Claro, joven?*"

"*Cristólino, viejo,*" Rafael promised through a wide, happy smile.

"*Bueno! Vaya con díos, niño.*"

He might have managed it. And the Fates might have played it differently for Rafael Bustámante, had he not departed Las Piedras by way of the bull pastures. The sight of those magnificent animals called to his heart. Their sheer animal, masculine power awed him, yet filled him with an emotion akin to lust. The thought of besting one of these most dangerous brutes sent a jolt through him with all the tingling sensitivity of a sexual climax.

"*Olé! Olé!*"

Rafael could hear the accolades and see a swarm of pretty young girls all around him. As they had done to him since the age of eight, the bulls gave Rafael a strident, painful erection, as sexual fantasies of what he and those girls would do together filled his head. Without conscious direction, Rafael wormed his way over the stone fence, unfurled his *capóte* and cited the nearest bull.

"Ah-ah! A-ha, *toro*. *Vien, toro*," Rafael chanted, suspended from reality by his erotic visions.

The bull in question, No. 37, *Tronidoro*, lowered his head and snorted in irritation. He pawed the sandy soil with one large hoof, which sent up a shower of dust that scattered the little black birds from his shoulders. From the forward corner of his vision, he saw movement and heard a high, clear sound he associated with the creatures with four legs, two heads and a pair of ridiculous looking side appendages.

"Ah-hah, *toro!*" Rafael shouted again.

This had gotten to be more irritation than any fighting bull should have to endure. With a chopped-off bellow, Thunderer launched into a graceful charge. Slow at first, it built to nearly twenty-five miles an hour within three body lengths. Charged with adrenaline, Rafael gauged his movements correctly and passed the giant creature in a serpentine motion along his body and around to the left. Guided by the visible corner of the cape, *Tronidoro* followed perfectly. Suddenly the moving, insulting cloth disappeared.

Tronidoro whirled and stopped.

"Ah-ha, *toro!*"

There it was again. Thunderer lived up to his name as he bore down on the waggling impudence. Closer now, closer. Confoundingly, it moved again. He swept past something insubstantial, bent toward the ground and twisted to the left once more.

"*¡Condenácion! Uno guitáno!*" A more familiar sound came from behind the enraged bull.

"*¡Hijo de la chingada, vayate!*" called another comfortable sound.

Rafael found himself facing two mounted, and quite angry, *váqueros*. Fleetingly he recalled the words of Eloy Herrada about staying out of sight and trouble. With a quick twist, he furled his *capóte* and ran like hell for the fence. A drum roll of hoofbeats told him the *váqueros* had taken up pursuit.

Chapter 5

Given his state of rage and all the rapidly moving objects, Thunderer didn't know which to attack first. He did manage to unhorse one rider and send the other loping for safety. In the excitement Rafael Bustámente cleared the wall in a single leap, without need of wriggling on his belly across the top. He fell into the arms of a third *váquero*, who pinned his arms to his skinny sides.

"Look at this!" he called out over Rafael's contralto objections. "*Un gallo.*"

"More like a *pollo*," Oscar Tampas answered him as he limped painfully from where he had been thrown.

"Ah, no, this one has *cójones*," Salvatore Lambras responded as he groped Rafael's crotch in a rough, hurtful manner. "He is a skinny *gallo*, but a rooster all the same."

"Keep your hand off my pecker," Rafael snarled at Lambras in the distinctive accent of Mexico City. With a hot flash of anger, Rafael recalled the uninvited and unwelcome familiarity to which he had sometimes been subjected over his early years as a *guitáno*. "If you try to force me, I'll bite the head off."

"Hey-hey-hey, *gallíto*, we were only making fun with

you. We're not that kind of *cabrones*. Those *putos* you find in the big cities. You understand?" Tampas queried. "It is to laugh, not a dirty thing. Now, we come to the real problem. You being here. You trespass on Las Piedras and you maybe ruin a good bull. We must take you to the *Patrón*."

Rafael's eyes went wide with fear. "Oh, no. Please don't do that. I — I'll leave and not cause any trouble. I promise."

"You are good at promises, I imagine," Lambras growled. "Eh, *guitáno*?"

"I swear," Rafael stated solemnly, making the sign of the cross despite being encumbered by Lambras' strong arms. "On the life of my mother and the grave of my father. I will not return here unless someone invites me," he added, thinking of how he satisfied the oath while keeping the old man's invitation secret.

"That is for the *Patrón* to decide. Come along." Lambras forked Rafael over the front of his saddle, swung up and cantered off. "Oscar, you two stay and calm the bulls. If this one says nothing, I will not mention you were dumped from your horse."

His jibe stung all the more, since Salvator Lambras was the *mayorál* of Las Piedras. "*En tu boca, Salvátor,*" Oscar riposted.

At the main house, the youthful *mayorál* took Rafael into a large, high-ceilinged study. There, in a uniform jacket and casual trousers, Pablo Ordaz listened to the account of Rafael's capture. He nodded occasionally, but asked no questions of the boy. When Lambras finished, Ordaz waved a casual hand.

"What should I do?"

"Let me give him a sound whipping with a willow switch. That's what's usually done," the *mayorál* suggested.

"Crude . . . but effective, eh? What do you think?" Ordaz inquired of a third party.

For the first time, Rafael saw the *gringo* sitting in a high, wing-back chair. He sipped from a brandy snifter, worked his full, sensual lips and licked them before answering. "You've caught him fair and square," Roger Styles began in excellent, if accented, Spanish.

"I suppose punishment is the next order. However . . . what about it, boy? Do you really want to get out there with those deadly animals?"

"*Sí, señor.* All of my life I have wanted to do so," Rafael answered earnestly, uncertain of the *gringo's* position, but hopeful of an ally.

"But you did trespass and you did cape one of the grown bulls?"

Rafael hung his head. "*Sí, señor. Tengo mucho verqüenzas.*"

"I'm not sure of how much shame you have acquired. But I think . . . and don't you agree, Pablo. In this instance, perhaps the punishment should fit the crime?"

Rafael sensed a subtle exchange between the two. It was as though the *gringo* was in fact the *Patrón* and this Federale officer his underling. He grew more confused when the supposed *Patrón* questioned the suggestion uncertainly.

"*Que?* How do you mean?"

"I suggest that if the lad wants a chance to try his skill, he should be given that chance."

"*De veras?*" Rafael blurted out excitedly. "Do you really mean that, *señor?*"

"Of course I do. In fact . . ." Roger drawled, "we might make you the star attraction at the *tienta.*"

Once again posing as Delawares, Rebecca and Whirlwind stopped off in Chadron, Nebraska, to make several purchases. The first was a wagon and team.

"Why such a run-down rolling lodge?" Whirlwind questioned when the proprietor of the wagon shop stepped out of earshot. "We could do much better."

"Yes. We could afford the best. But no one will expect such a vehicle to be carrying valuable cargo," Rebecca advised him. "The same for the mules. It doesn't matter if they're swaybacked and a bit old. Once we've accomplished our purpose, they can be disposed of."

Whirlwind grinned. "Eaten? What else? Who would want to trade for them?"

Rebecca grimaced. "We'll worry about that later. Now we have to outfit our 'stock in trade' for the, ah, 'trading post'."

Their purchases included a hundred blankets, thick and warm ones in bright, solid colors, two barrels of sugar and a hundred pound sack of roasted coffee beans, thirty large, deep cast iron dutch ovens, and forty Remington rifles. The ammunition, Rebecca decided, would be purchased elsewhere. While the merchant and his two strapping teen-aged sons loaded the wagon, Rebecca and Whirlwind stood to one side.

"You did not get a Winchester," Whirlwind accused. "Not even one for me. Don't I deserve a good rifle for showing you the gold?"

"That isn't the point," Rebecca snapped. But how could she tell him what truly bothered her? How could she say she feared that with a Winchester repeater, he might become arrogant around white soldiers? The

57

superior weapon would encourage that sort of attitude for any Sioux warrior.

"It is for me."

Whirlwind pushed out his lower lip. For a moment it reminded Rebecca of Joey. Unreasoningly, she wanted to take Whirlwind by the shoulders and shake him until his teeth rattled. Their by-play ended then as the merchant came over, dusting his hands together.

"You made a mighty good deal there," he declared. "Tell the chief he's a shrewd bargainer."

For the storekeeper's benefit, Whirlwind had been introduced as a Delaware sub-chief and Rebecca his squaw-interpreter. She continued the ruse, speaking to Whirlwind in Lakota, confident the white man could not discern the difference between it and any Indian tongue.

"Yep," the merchant went on. "There's lots of your people out there workin' as contract hunters. They surely favor those Remingtons for buffalo guns. You'll double your money, I'll wager," he added with a conspiratorial wink.

"If we don't lose it all," Rebecca told him. "There are many who would make their living taking from others."

"Ummm. You've got a point. Where'd you say this tradin' post of yours is located?"

"I didn't," Rebecca answered simply.

"Uh, well, ah, would you be interested in some fine calico cloth? I've a shipment coming in soon. You folks have done a lot of business with me and I'd allow you a special price."

"We might do that next trip. Thank you for everything you've done," Rebecca signaled an end to the exchange.

After the Delaware couple started out, the woman

58

driving the wagon, the man leading on horseback, the owner of the mercantile stared after them. He felt a little ill at ease over the sale of so many rifles. After all, these half-breeds had been known to run guns to the hostiles. But what the hell, he was a businessman, not a U.S. marshal. A sale was a sale.

For two days the invited guests had been arriving at Las Piedras. The *ganadería* buzzed with excitement. The *Patrón* had prepared a huge feast for the first serious *tienta* of the year. Rumor had it that he would allow a young *guitáno* to participate. One caught in with the mature bulls. Few among those gathered had the slightest idea that Coronel Pablo Ordaz was not in fact the master of Las Piedras. He only fronted for Roger Styles. The reason was simple.

With all the jealous assiduity of a religious hierarchy, the inner circle of *ganáderos*, both in Spain and Mexico, guarded the precious product of their enterprise. No outsider, of any other nationality had owned a bull ranch in Spain or Mexico. Not even a Mexican would be permitted to run a *ganadería* in Spain. Thus, when Roger expressed his desire to become one of these most revered of landowners, everyone tried to dissuade him.

At last, *Presidente* Diaz suggested a solution. Unpaid "taxes" were found for Las Piedras, and huge debts for supplies that never existed. Forced out of his family's three generation holding, the owner saw his treasured ranch sold at auction to Coronel Pablo Ordaz. The money came from Roger Styles. All the same, it was Ordaz who publicly played the grand host. A more somber note fell on the crowd on the final day before the *tienta*, when a company of Federales, Lancers under command of Lt. Xavier Alvarado, rode in, escorting Hector Blancos, now a major, and the hefty former Sergeant Mendoza, who wore the insignia of a captain.

Pablo Ordaz, resplendent in an expensive civilian suit, greeted them at the *hacienda*. When the young lieutenant gave the orders to dismount, find quarters for the horses and themselves, it became evident that the soldiers had not come to arrest anyone. Like the other guests, they were here to enjoy the spectacle and the feast to follow.

"Come in, come in," Ordaz boomed cordially. "I have had a light repast laid out to refresh you from your journey."

In the high-ceilinged dining room of the thick-walled rectangular structure, built around an open, interior courtyard, a long table had been set with fine linen and heavy silver. Ice, brought at great expense from the Sierra Madres, chilled bottles of wine and large ollas of *refrescos*, steeped decoctions of tamarind pods, cinnamon bark and crushed berries. Vigas of carefully smoothed soft woods covered the ceiling between open thirty foot beams fully twelve by twenty inches in size. Roger Styles, and three other *gringos* — imported ruffians in his personal pay — joined the Mexicans there.

"Get something to drink and be seated," Roger commenced, not at all hesitant about taking charge. "We have a lot to discuss."

"I gather that you and Pablo have been busy, eh, *Señor* Styles?" Hector Blancos observed.

"That we have," Roger answered lightly. "First off, I'd like a report on how you are progressing in collecting the, ah, 'contributions' from the other landholders?"

"It goes well," Hector answered. "Some scream and call it extortion, but the threat of a rope or a bullet usually brings quick cooperation. They even believe that this is a general government policy. And that," he nodded toward Pablo Ordaz, "even the military governor is not exempt. With such a grand holding as this, they're sure you must *pagar un precio exorbitante*."

"*Que bueño!* Pay through the nose, is it?" Pablo snorted through a laugh. "As long as they continue to think so, we'll have no trouble, eh?"

"Good," Roger concluded the item. "To move on, I have excellent news from the capital. The application for a railroad has been approved. We can begin construction on the spur at once. The Minister of Home Affairs has granted us a five hectare wide right of way on each side of the track. We can develop the land as we see fit, or sell it once the line is completed."

"*¡Chingada!* That means we are all rich, Roger," Ordaz shouted. "This calls for something stronger than tamarindo. Pepe, bring the tequíla!"

"There's one more item," Roger injected before the meeting degenerated into a drinking and eating contest. "You may call this a personal vendetta, yet I believe it necessary. Chris, you've done well in obtaining these two men. *Señores*, let me introduce Chris Starret, Hank Bridger and Anson Angleton."

Christopher Starret pushed back the brim of his black, low-crowned hat to reveal a wide expanse of bare scalp. His long face and cold gray eyes eloquently proclaimed his profession as a gunhand. Seated at the far end of the table, lean and hard as a pair of bookends, Henry Bridger and Anson Angleton nodded silent acknowledgment of the introduction.

"I've got one more lined up, Roger. Harry Gonzales-Gonzales. He's in Paso del Norte. He's laid up with a dose of the trots," Chris informed Roger.

"Too bad. Perhaps by the time you get there, he'll be able to travel. What I want you to do is head north, recruit as you go. I need twelve good guns. You're to ride to Dakota Territory. There's a woman there, Rebecca Caldwell. I want you to find her and bring her here to me. You're not to kill her, mind. Just bring her in alive."

"What if we have to rough her up some?" Chris inquired, a slight lilt of foreign accent in his words.

"As long as you don't kill her, you can do as you please. Bring the men you enlisted along with you. They will serve as my personal bodyguard and, under your direction, Chris, as a special elite force to keep these locals in line."

"When do we leave?" Chris asked.

"Immediately after the fiesta," Roger told him.

Chapter 6

Violins and guitars, a bass and silvery trumpets set the air ashiver. A carnival mood swept through the two small villages that were a part of Las Piedras holdings. The people, who were beholden to the *Patrón* for their livelihood, were gearing up to enjoy to the fullest the fiesta that would follow the *tienta*. Such occasions were rare in their lives, usually numbering no more than three a year. Lt. Xavier Alvarado y Polanski and his troops soon became caught up in the holiday.

"*Teniente,* with your permission?" whippet-thin Sgt. Paco Alvarez called out to him as the NCO danced away in the arms of a sloe-eyed beauty.

"Go ahead, Alvarez. Show the ladies how Lancers dance," the young officer answered laughingly. Someone offered him a clay bottle of tequila. "*Grácias.*"

It burned a trail down Alvarado's throat, which reminded him of his father's admonition to confine oneself to the taking of wine or beer only. But *que el diáblo,* this was a party like none he had ever seen before. Three moderately attractive young girls, who normally patted out corn cakes in the local *tortillária,* began a lively flamenco dance on a low wooden platform. A crowd quickly gathered, swelled by the appreciative

Lancers. Grinning hugely, Xavier worked his way to the front.

Enraptured by the swirling skirts and flashes of bare leg, time passed quickly for the healthy young soldiers. There would be feasting that night, and much drinking, Lt. Alvarado reminded himself. Then, in the morning, after a lazy breakfast, everyone would troop out the short distance to the *tienta* ring, where the testing would begin after a midday repast of cold roast meat, cheeses, fruit and bread. Perhaps, Alvarado considered for a moment, the *gringo*, Styles, was not so bad after all.

With a loud whoop, the warriors, women and children of the Red Top Lodge band swept down on the cache. Pots and blankets were doled out, according to the needs of each lodge. Whirlwind had banished his own pique long enough to proudly pass out the Remington rifles to each man in the village. Rebecca had bought enough so that even the older youths had new hunting pieces. That included one special rifle, a Marlin No. 4 Perfection in .32-40, for *Pinzpinzala*. Handling it again brought back a flash of resentment to Whirlwind, when he recalled his special request had been denied.

Then the youngster unabashedly hugged Whirlwind and thanked him profusely, believing the gift had been the warrior's idea, not that of his stepmother. The open, unrestrained love Joey offered touched Whirlwind and cooled his resentment. He gave the boy a box of bright new cartridges and the simple Lyman loading tool and bullet mold it would require to maintain a supply of ammunition. That had been his idea. Even the great Crazy Horse had loading equipment, considered routine necessity by those familiar with firearms. Quickly, after the issue of the rifles, the gathering began to break up.

Chattering women and gleeful children set off in family groups for the distant village. A cluster of admiring youngsters swarmed around *Pinzpinzala,* reluctant to depart with their elders, eager to see the superb new rifle. When only a few remained, Whirlwind came to Rebecca.

"You were right about the rifles. At least it looks like that now," he told her bluntly.

"Oh? What changed your mind?" Rebecca countered.

"The men seem so happy with what they have," he mused aloud. "I would think they'd want repeating rifles."

"Not if they weren't promised them in the first place," Rebecca said a bit smugly. "Besides, the Remingtons are more powerful and accurate."

Whirlwind bristled. "Are you . . . ?" He paused, let the temper pass. "Will we camp here?"

"I thought so. It's getting late and I want to fix a good meal for you and *Pinzpinzala.* Besides, I'm getting to be rather fond of this Delaware disguise. When everything is removed to camp, what say we go off on a little hunting expedition, as Delawares?"

"What about *Pinzpinzala?*" Whirlwind asked.

"He can come or stay with Tall Elk. After all, isn't that the Oglala way?" she ended teasingly. "Besides, think of the fun we could have without him."

Business concluded, and a night of partying behind

them, Roger moved his principal guests out to the arena, to witness a "spectacle" as he put it. The *tienta* ring, and the large, adobe block section of stands, glowed in a bright morning sun. Fresh flowers had been cut and placed in colorfully decorated bowls and hanging baskets. Flags and bunting rippled in the wind, red-white-green, the colors of Mexico. A *mariachi* band entertained the early arrivals. The peons, children mostly, sat atop the high outer wall that circled the sandy arena. The stands were divided into three levels.

At ground level, those honored by an invitation to participate waited. Somewhat nervously, they checked their capes, the condition of their boot soles, the precise tilt of their low-crowned circular cut Sávilla sombreros of pearl grey, russet and bright green. These matched the bolero jackets and tight trousers of their *traje de corta,* or ranch costumes. On the second level sat the lesser guests, who brought their own food and drink. Above, with a clear view of everything, the important personages gathered. They sipped chilled sparkling water, from the natural lithia springs to the south in the mountains, nibbled on pungent cheeses, apples and grapes. Hot bread, and *pan dulce* made the air redolent with savory odors. Excitement grew as the time wore on.

At last, Pablo Ordaz raised a white handkerchief to signal the two trumpeters seated behind the rows of spectators in the upper gallery. They rose and sounded the *clarín*. At once silence descended. Seven men, dressed in their ranch finery, marched onto the sand and presented themselves to the *Patrón*. Led by seventeen year old Pedro Dominguez, an aspiring young *matador*, they ranged in age up to a favored *viéjo* of sixty-five. No sign of the rumored *guitáno* as yet. The large gate across the arena opened and two men entered, mounted on padded horses.

On their right legs they wore the cotton quilt-bolstered armor of picadors, with canvas trousers, soft shirts and leather jackets. Small round hats, which reminded Roger Styles of Sancho Panza in *Don Quixote,* sat on their heads. Each carried a long wooden lance, with a sturdy stop-ring near the end. The pic tips, for this occasion no larger than a small person's little finger, flashed diamond highlights from the sun. At a signal from Ordaz, the entire group dispersed behind the *barrera* fence.

With another call of the *clarín,* the first small, six month old heifer bolted into the arena. Hoots of laughter and jeers followed as the skittery creature's hind legs tried valiantly to catch up with the front. A young man from a neighboring ranch stepped out and spread his *capóte.* Two skillful passes brought the calf to the picador. The short, sharp tip entered skin and muscle on the heifer's right shoulder.

A brief, strident bellow followed, much like the yell of a man stung by a bee. The picador leaned his considerable weight on the lance and worried it in the wound until the heifer bellowed again. Then he relaxed his pose and withdrew the pic as the youth came forward for the *quité.* Attracted by the moving cape, the *vácilla* turned from the horse and charged.

Two wide passes, a close-in *reboléra* and finally a *medío veroníca* sent the spunky calf back to the pic. She took it in good form. Forgotten now were her antics upon entering. The spectators showed their appreciation of her courage.

"*Ole, vácilla!*"

Ay, vacá, show them all up!"

Eyes locked on the young animal, the *mayoral* and *segundo* took meticulous notes on her performance. After two more pickings, the *mayoral*, Salvatór Lambras, signaled for the *váqueros* to bulldog her and take her out. As usual, this performance brought chuckles from the audience. Five or six grown men attempting to take down a small calf, without hurting it, or being harmed. A relatively informal affair, compared to a *noviada,* or a formal *corrida,* the *tienta* dispensed with *clarín* calls for each event. The *mayoral* gave his signal and the next calf entered.

Lambras and the *segundo* turned to the page with the animal's brand number and began to take notes. Another of the adventurous stepped onto the sand and began passes with the *vácilla.* The crowd began to cheer or jeer, depending on the performance of man and beast. After seven or more small calves had taken their turns, larger, year old, and *muy sabe vacás* entered to contest the lance.

The bellows were louder, the charges faster and the occasional impact with horse or man considerably more violent. One picador, who had been clowning for the audience, nearly lost his seat when a hefty *vacá* slammed into the padding that protected his horse. That brought greater laughter than his earlier antics. Between test animals, a small murmur rippled through the crowd. What of the *guitáno* boy? The afternoon wore on.

Following the six yearlings larger, ready for breeding heifers of eighteen months age took their turns. This would be the most critical judging of all. Every one of the seven professional and skilled amateur *taurínos* took a turn with each *váca.* One went to the pic five times at

68

the direction of the *mayoral*. At last the sand emptied. *Mozos,* the maintenance crew, called "monkeys," quickly swept the rough ground into shape and removed animal droppings. Boys in their early teens, they wore bright red jackets and pillbox hats. They yelled jesting insults at each other as they worked.

Unaccountably, the *clarín* sounded again, as they exited. Pablo Ordaz rose and spoke loudly to the gathered spectators. "Gentlemen and ladies, at the suggestion of the personal envoy of *Presidente* Díaz, we have an unusual end to the *tienta.* Following the next event, we will repair to enjoy the fiesta prepared for our pleasure. First, a little background.

"We are all aware of the sometimes depredations caused by the *guitános.* They ruin bulls, create stampedes, or have the bad grace to die in one of our pastures." Chuckles followed Ordaz's remarks. "Recently my *mayoral* apprehended a young *guitáno,* a boy called Rafael Bustámante. We sought to find some family and return him. Alas, there were no results. The boy seems sincere in his desire to try his skill with the cape. So, at the behest of the president's envoy, today we give him that opportunity."

"Diós mió, no!" an aged voice choked out quietly from the stock pens. Eloy Herrara had wondered why the large, vicious old *váca,* Esmirálda, so cape-wise and dangerous, had been brought up out of pasture for today. Now he knew. The boy, such a sweet child, would have no chance at all. To his shame, Eloy realized the crowd thought otherwise.

Slightly bibulous after the long afternoon, they shouted approval as the *clarín* sounded again. Rafael Bustámante, who had until then been kept in a small, dark room found himself thrust out onto the sand.

Someone handed him his *capóte* and stepped behind a *burladéro* as the gate to the stock alley swung wide. A huge, black and gray, powerfully built cow lumbered out, eyes red and wild, streams of mucus slobbering from flared nostrils. Reacting to shouts and cheers, and the flicking of capes over the edge of the barrier, she pounded to full speed and raced around the ring, toward Rafael.

Numb and confused, the lad belatedly unfurled his *capóte* and grasped it in the proper manner. Stiffly he executed a wide *veronica*. Spatters of applause answered his half-hearted effort. The *váca* wheeled and thundered back at him.

He steadied himself, observing how the *moríl*, at the withers, slid past above his eye level. *Por diós*, what a monster. His third pass smoothed out even more. Heart pounding, Rafael began to believe he could in fact master this huge beast. He set his feet, cited her, teased with the left skirt of his cape. Esmirálda bellowed in rage and plunged toward him.

Too late, Rafael saw that her eyes set too far forward in her head, that she didn't have the usual blind spot most bovines bred for this purpose possess. He swung wide and vaulted the *barréra*. First to his side was old Eloy Herrada, who picked him up while the *váca* slammed wicked horns into the thick wooden planks.

"Her name is Esmirálda. She is *loco. Muy sabe* of the cape. Make a few wide passes, then get out of there and run far and fast. *Vaya con diós, niño.*"

"Help me," Rafael pleaded, knowing he was far beyond his ability.

"I cannot. Only God can help you now," Eloy answered, tears in his eyes.

"Get him back in there, goddamnit," Chris Starret

growled from the stand above.

Squaring his shoulders, Rafael walked to the nearest *burladero* and stepped back on the sand. Esmirálda charged instantly. With a deft twist and sidestep pivot, Rafael directed her into solid, head-aching contact with the *barréra*. Esmirálda bellowed and threatened to jump the barrier. The *clarín* sounded and a single picador entered. He had a larger tip on his lance, though not so big as those used on adult bulls. Rafael saw his positioning, gauged distances and cited the *váca*.

At once she showered sand skyward and loped toward the frightened boy. He managed a series of three connected passes, then delivered her onto the pic. Face pale, biting his lower lip, the young *matador*, Pedro Dominguez, stepped out to take the first *quité*. As he passed Rafael, he spoke in a whisper.

"This should not be happening. I am sorry. Let me tire her a little, then set her up for another pic. High, near the *morîl*. Indicate it to the picador."

Dominguez proceeded to do as he said. In the midst of his brilliant, though difficult, performance, the *clarín* sounded again. No second pic.

"Take the sticks, boy," a voice snarled from behind Rafael. "You'll place all three sets."

"But, I've never . . ." Rafael started to protest.

"Too bad. You should train better before a fight."

Of a sudden, Rafael had the crowd behind him. Their shouts of *olé* rang across the arena. His heart had steadied, and charged with adrenaline, he began to take new courage. With a *bandarillá* in each hand, he hefted the gaily decorated sticks with the wicked barbed tips. Arms extended upward, the bases of the *bandarillás* against his palms, fingers grasping the clear portion of the shafts, he began a pigeon-toed, serpen-

71

tine walk in front of the panting, slobbering *váca*.

"High," Dominguez shouted to him. "High and on the right. Second set high left."

Esmirálda noticed him, came alert, hackles risen. Tail switching, she bellowed a challenge. Hoofs alternately pawed the sand. Rafael came closer. The audience held a terrible silence. Then the *váca* charged. Rafael started his run, high on tip-toes. At the last moment, he launched himself off the ground and planted the barbs in Esmirálda's right side.

"*¡Olé! ¡Olé! ¡Olé! ¡Ma-ta-dor! ¡Ma-ta-dor!*" The crowd went wild.

Rafael, dizzy with the rush of unexpected success, sped to the *barrerá* and accepted a second set. "High and left?" he questioned.

"Yes. Be careful, you little fool," Dominguez warned.

Alive with his power, Rafael began his zigzag walk again. His body swayed, hips swiveled, arms swung left and right, softly he cooed to the deadly beast. Called to her to come to him. She sensed the enemy, snorted and turned to face her foe. Blood streamed down from the single pic wound in the right shoulder and the barbs above it. Sand flew from under a front hoof. Rafael drew closer. He paused. Jumped up and down and shouted.

Esmirálda charged. Rafael rose to his fullest height and sprang into the air. The *bandarillás* descended, bit into flesh. And Rafael came down onto the up-slanted tip of Esmirálda's left horn.

Impaled through the abdomen, fiery pain howling in his body, Rafael didn't even notice the ferocious shaking the *váca* gave him. Flung about like a rag doll, though still attached to the horn, Rafael's body looked almost comical until he shook free and dropped to the

72

ground, spurting a great gout of blood. Twice more, before Pedro Dominguez and two skilled attendants could reach him, Esmirálda pierced Rafael's body with thick, splinter-tipped horns. Screams of horror came from the women. The men struggled to rescue the boy.

When at last the old cow was distracted from her prize, they dragged a corpse off the sand and hoisted the pitifully gored body to shoulders. Saddened, they started out. Lt. Xavier Alvarado looked on in stunned disbelief. Murmurs of discontent ran among his troops. The bandit guests appeared to love the brutal murder. Anger rose. Mexico should not have to live with such shame, Xavier fumed. Above him, in the upper box, a different attitude prevailed.

Glassy-eyed, Roger Styles started after the dead boy. He felt total exhilaration when the horn entered that tender flesh. From the sounds rising from the lower class, he sensed approval. Tribute to a savage heart from a hundred others. Truly he had found his place in life.

73

Chapter 7

Laughter rolled from the open doors of the Paso del Norte saloon. High, shrill, feminine giggles joined deep masculine guffaws. The source of this mirth evaded the three dusty riders until they reined in and dismounted. Chris Starret, Hank Bridger and Anse Angleton slapped dust from their shirts and trousers, replaced their hats at jaunty angles and clumped across the board porch to the recessed batwings that afforded token privacy to the barroom beyond. Peering over the gracefully curved top of the louvered partitions, Chris first spotted the reason for such hilarity.

Crouched on hands and knees, on a green baize poker table, looking ever so much like the bulldog his features resembled, Harry Gonzalès-Gonzales lunged at a bunch of grapes. Held in the hand of an above average looking saloon girl, who stood on a neighboring table, the globular fruit inscribed circles and figure eights in the air over Harry's head. With each snap of his jaws, Harry would remove a few more grapes. It elicited peals of mirth from the other patrons.

"Harry, what the hell are you doing?" Chris roared.

The human bulldog stopped his antics and peered toward the door. When he recognized the owner of the strident voice, he scrambled off the table and swept up his hat, a large charro sombrero, and held it before his chest.

"Oh, hello, Señor Chrees. I deed not know it was chu," he declared breathlessly.

"The doggie act, Harry. What's it all about?"

"Oh, that. She say if I eat all the grapes, she let me be her lap dog and lap at her, aaah, chu know what, Chris, no? An' that we make love for free."

"You may be well, but you're broke as usual, eh, Harry?"

"*Sí*. Eet is—how you say?—a habit weeth me. Also, I am *muy* horny, so . . . well, where there is a weel there is a way, *como no?*"

"We're ridin', Harry," Chris said coldly.

"Oh." Harry waited a long silent moment. "Where an' what for?"

"I'll tell you that later. Now, collect your gear and meet us back here, with a saddled horse, in one hour."

"Hookay-dookay, Señor Chrees. Uh . . . only, I done sol' my horse," Harry added apologetically.

"Christ! How do I get myself into these things? I'll get you a horse, Harry. Just be back here in one hour, ready to go. Uh, what about a saddle?"

"I nevair sell the fine Sonora saddle, Chrees," Harry drew himself up with pride, then added in a beseeching tone. "Chu know thees."

Cocks crowed over the small community of Las Cruces, in the newly created State of New Mexico. Pastel bands softly lighted the eastern horizon. Save for Padre Ignacius, who puttered about the kitchen of his small quarters beside the church, drinking a final cup of coffee before preparations for morning mass, all the good folks of Las Cruces slept soundly. That did not include the local bad man, Juan Valdez, nor the short, curly haired *Anglo* who stood quietly drinking at the far end of the bar in the Cantina El Sol. Unfortunately, that also meant the bartender, Lupe Perez had to remain awake long after the usual ten o'clock closing time.

Truth to tell, Lupe feared Valdez and felt no less secure with the prospect of displeasing the *gringo.* Valdez's snarl sent tremors along Lupe's spine.

"Cantiñero."

"P-perhaps some coffee, *Jéfe?"* Lupe quaveringly suggested.

"Estupído! I piss in your coffee. No real man drinks coffee when there's tequila at hand. Bring me another bottle."

"Perhaps you should listen to him," the quiet Americano suggested softly. "You're getting pretty drunk, you know. And, ah, I'll have a cup of coffee, *cantiñero."*

"Keep out of this, *gringo cabrón,"* Valdez growled.

"My, my. Such temper,. Really it isn't nice to call people bad names. Especially when you don't know them very well."

The *gringo's* words had hardened slightly, yet only the sober barkeep caught the menace behind them. He sidled along the bar to fetch a cup of coffee. Truth to be told, Lupe would rather be in the next room, with the cookstove, than anywhere near these two.

"Are you insulting me? Me, *gringo?"* Valdez rumbled.

"No insult meant. I'm only giving advice," the humble voice returned.

"Take your advice somewhere else," Valdez snarled. "Leave, get out of here. Your face offends me."

A mocking smile flickered on the Anglo's face. "Now it's you who is being insulting."

"Miérde! Everywhere you go these days, it's *gringos,*

76

gringos, gringos. I tell you to leave as a favor, *gringo.* For if you do not, I will keel you."

"You wouldn't have a chance." A flat, direct statement, filled with a ringing confidence.

"Hijo de la chingada! Don' you know me? I am Juan Valdez. I am one *malo hombre.* Strong men quake at mention of my name."

"I'm Luke Nelson, and I'm terribly unimpressed."

"You are a dead man, *gringo.*"

Juan Valdez's hand dropped to his holstered revolver. Luke Nelson reached behind his head. As though by twinkling magic, a knife appeared in Luke's hand. He whipped it forward and released. The keen edge cut hypnotic lines in the golden lamplight. Before Valdez cleared leather, the tip bit flesh in the hollow of his throat. Momentum carried the full length of the blade into his neck. Massive, mind-numbing shock released Juan's hold on the hard rubber grips of his Colt sixgun and it clattered to the floor. Frozen in place, the bartender started to speak when the door flew open.

"Hello, Chris," Luke Nelson said mildly, over the sound of the body hitting the floor.

"I thought I'd find you here," Chris replied. "You have anything that's holdin' you in these parts, Luke?"

Luke studied the final death throes of Juan Valdez, crossed and retrieved his knife, wiping it on the dead man's shirt. "Nope."

"It pays well. Tell you about it on the way."

Albuquerque, New Mexico, all of it, clustered around a large, tree-shaded Plaza de Armas. On one side the cathedral rose majestically into the pale blue sky. At the center, a fountain offered cooling surcease to man and beast. Barefoot children splashed in it, laughing and cavorting between the legs of adults and horses. Jays scolded from the trees. Across the plaza, next to the seat of civil authority, the jail looked squat and forbidding. The symbolism of this juxtaposition of the secular and ecclesiastical power was lost on nearly all of the residents. A weathered, sun-faded sign above the door to the jail identified it in English and Spanish.

Behind the *carcel*, Chris Starret and Anse Angleton found a square, muscular man, with the hawk-nosed features of his quarter-Indian ancestry. Hampered by leg irons, he worked at splitting small piñon logs into firewood. From long practice, his axe never broke its rhythmic *chunk-chunk*, even when he spoke.

"A fellow . . ." *Chunk!* "wouldn't expect . . ." *Chunk!* "to see you . . ." *Chunk!* "in a place . . ." *Chunk!* "like this, Chris."

"You can quit that now, Jim," Chris stated in his slight lilt of foreign accent.

Chunk! "Oh?"

"I paid your fine."

Jim Elkhorn set aside the axe and pulled a face. His words came out dissemblingly. "Oh, that. It was too trifling to bother with. I had the money to pay it." He shrugged. "Only, it made me so gol-danged mad. How can a man be arrested, hauled into court and fined for plantin' something on his own land?"

"How's Mari and the children?" Chris changed the subject.

"Fine. Fine as can be, what with their man off in jail for plantin' fruit trees when Mister High and Mighty Hotchkiss wants to have the only orchard in this whole valley. Did you know that was my crime? Did you, Chris?"

"You've got three fine boys there. They need their father at home, Jim."

"Four. We've got four now," Jim answered. "Chris, I

78

know you. You didn't pay my fine so I could go back to my family."

Chris produced a hint of a smile. "I've got a job for you. We've got to pick someone up in Dakota Territory, a girl, and take her to my, ah, client in Mexico."

"No, Chris. Oh, no. I've only got a week to go and I'll be back with my Mari and the boys. You find yourself another gunhand."

"I *want* you, Jim. You're among the best. Nearly as good as me. Without you, we can't pull it off."

Squint lines made gullies of Jim Elkhorn's face. "How much?"

"A thousand, and expenses."

Chris' words dropped like stones. In the momentary silence, Anse Angleton turned all of his sour suspicion on Jim Elkhorn. Arrogant son of a bitch, Anse fumed. He'll probably still refuse, just to make it hard for the rest of us. His narrow, pinched face, with the hint of a receding chin and over-large crown gave his head an oddly triangular appearance. Innate bitterness and distrust of everyone had enhanced the effect. He hated people who laughed freely, like this Jim Elkhorn. They had to be up to something sneaky, hidden behind a mask of open friendliness.

"Awh, Chris, Chris. You know all the right words. You could con the birds outta the trees. For that kind of cash money I could fix up that dump we're livin' in and make my land pay right handsome. When do we leave?"

"Sunup, tomorrow," Chris answered tersely.

Larks warbled in the tall grass that trailed behind. The long slope, which grew rockier with each half-dozen strides, led toward Raton Pass. Colorado lay beyond and fed Chris Starret's hopes. Santa Fe had been a bust, as had Taos. Not a hardcase worthy of the name to be found. Recruit a dozen men. Hell, he had only seven now. Ahead, the huge, rounded face of a tall bluff sent the trail bending out of sight. The grade would increase sharply from there on.

"We'll get into the shade of the pass, then give the horses a blow," Chris informed the six men riding with him.

" 'Bout time," Anse Angleton complained. "My stomach thinks my throat's been cut."

Beyond the big granite bluff that marked the lower end of Raton Pass, Chris and the others came up sharply, confronted by the large, black holes of a pair of Colt .45 muzzles. A baby-faced youngster, hat tipped back on his head at a jaunty angle, faced them. He wore thin, black, pigskin gloves, the tips cut from the fingers, black leather vest and trousers, and an off-white shirt without a collar, which had seen better days. It took Chris several tense seconds to realize the youth had thumbs tightly set over the hammers. Also that Harry Gonzales-Gonzales was no longer with the group.

"Whoa. Easy there, gentlemen. No offense meant, and no threat. From the looks of y'all, I'd say you," he pointed at Chris, "are Chris Starret. Word around is that you're looking for a few good men. Thought I'd take the opportunity to show you just how good I am. Th'name's Tibbs, Kid Tibbs." He back-rolled the revolvers and dumped them into their holsters. "I'm here to join up," he added unnecessarily.

"Tibbs," Chris mouthed speculatively. "I've heard of you. Little Jerry Tibbs, Terror of Moline, Kansas. You'd better go back home, grow out of your diapers and learn some manners before bracing your betters, Jerry."

Ice formed in Tibbs' big, wide-set brown eyes. A

shock of black hair fell over his high, smooth forehead. He must be, Chris calculated, all of nineteen, going on twelve.

"Gosh, Mister Starret, you've got no call to bad-mouth me like that," Tibbs responded in a whine-edged tone.

"You're the one who jumped us, boy," Chris said coldly.

"How 'bout that? Pretty good ambush, wasn't it?"

"Not really," Chris answered Tibbs levelly.

Defensive, Tibbs relied on brag. "I'll bet I coulda got you all."

"Chu lose, Keed," Harry Gonzales-Gonzales declared from behind the youthful outlaw.

A gale of laughter rose from the seven hardcases. Face flaming, Jerry Tibbs stood aside while the hard-faced gunhawks cantered past him. He watched them out of sight in the pass. Then Kid Tibbs cursed foully, spat on the ground and kicked a rock. His last show of anger provided him an exceedingly sore toe.

"Welcome to Colorado Springs," Anse Angleton mouthed bitterly. "This place ain't big enough to have a decent pot to piss in. Why're we stoppin' here, Chris?"

"To talk to two men," Chris answered practically.

"We don't need them," Anse protested. "There's seven of us. We can do the job. The more you get the less you can trust them."

"Why don't you leave that for *me* to decide?" Chris hissed, his voice alone a menace.

In the best saloon in town, there were only three, Chris instructed his men to take places along the bar and keep watch on everything and everyone. He took a seat in a shadowed corner and began to lay out a game of patience on the green baize of a poker table. A quarter of an hour later, the tall, glass-inleted doors opened to admit a stoop-shouldered man.

Nervous eyes zig zagged to register everything in the saloon. Then he sidled toward Chris, whipped off his hat and reached for a chair. "It's been a long time, hasn't it, Chris?"

His nose ran and his red-rimmed eyes watered. He nervously licked his lips and drew out the chair. "Mind if I sit?"

"Go ahead, Martin. Though you won't be here long."

Martin Dean brightened. "We ride right away, is that it?"

"Martin, I wouldn't take you to a dog fight. You've lost it. That special edge that makes the difference between a first class shootest and a stumblebum with a gun isn't there any more, Martin. I came to see Quinn and Davidson. Have you seen them around?"

Red suffused Martin Dean's face. "You've always had it in for me, Chris. You can't stand it that you're a skinhead and I've still got all mine, and not a white hair in the lot. You're jealous because you can't even grow a moustache. Why, I wouldn't ride with your outfit if you paid a thousand dollars up front."

"That's what I am paying, Martin. And you're still not riding."

Two hours later, both Quinn and Davidson had visited Chris at the shadowy table and agreed to join up. The growing gang rode out, headed toward Dodge City.

Chapter 8

Heat waves rippled the air as they rose from the flat, hard ground. It distorted the shapes of Spanish Bayonet, rabbits, and the few spavined cows along the main east-west road into Dodge City, Kansas. Wrapped in the concealing aberration, the gang halted at Chris Starret's signal.

"What is it, Boss?" Connor Quinn asked.

"You boys ride on in to town. I want to check something out," Chris answered.

"Need some help?" Hank Bridger offered.

"No, Hank. Someone's been dogging our trail all the way from the top of Raton Pass. I want to drop back and find out who and why. I'll join you at the Long Branch."

"Phaw!" Luke Nelson exploded out of his accustomed silence. "All those Kansas sodbusters serve up is beer. *Weak* beer at that."

"Not if you know the right people, Luke," Chris assured him. "Now, go on."

Twenty minutes later, Jerry Tibbs plodded into view. Chin on his chest, his head bobbed in rhythm to his mount's gait. Heat-lulled into a drowse, he jerked blinkingly awake at the sound of a sixgun hammer

83

racheting.

"Bang! You're dead," Chris chortled.

"Ga'dang ya, Chris. You caught me unfair," Tibbs protested.

"Not by my rules. What are you doing following us?"

"I . . . well, I, ah, figured you'd be needin' me sooner or later, Chris. So I decided to tag along. When the right time came, I'd move in."

"If you are that damned determined, I suppose you might as well ride *with* us as to eat our dust."

Jerry Tibbs brightened. "Ya mean I'm in? You're takin' me on?"

"At half the offered price and on a probationary status only," Chris admonished him.

"I'll take it. Goll-ee. Kid Tibbs ridin' with Chris Starret an' the meanest gunhands anywhere. What's the job, Boss?"

Chris groaned. "We're taking a girl—a young lady really—to Mexico."

Reality took the beaming glow from Tibbs' moon face. "Is that all? No range war? No sheepmen to shoot up? No towns to tame?"

"You wanted in, you're in. Take it or leave it," Chris said blandly.

"I'll take it, I'll take it," Jerry hastened to babble.

Hunting and loving, both had been plentiful. Long forgotten, the quarrel over the Winchester had been laid to rest. Rebecca Caldwell Ridgeway and Whirlwind basked in a warm glow of contentment. Rebecca was even on the point of agreeing that Wolf Brother should bind them with the sacred words. A wagon piled high with jerked meat and pliable hides went a long way toward a mellow, optimistic mood. Still in the guise of a Delaware couple, their journey from the Black Hills had been uneventful. Only a few miles separated them from the Rosebud Agency. A long ribbon of dust, curling up from a close-by ravine halted them abruptly.

"It could be some of Standing Bear's band, or ours, out hunting," Rebecca speculated.

"Or soldiers," Whirlwind suggested, seizing on the worst possible answer.

"They would be no threat to us. Remember, we're peaceful Delaware traders. No one is illegally off the reservation."

A ghost smile came and went on Whirlwind's thick lips. "You make it all sound so easy."

"We'll know soon enough," Rebecca observed, her eyes on the approaching plumes of brown.

Fifteen mounted riders crested the lip of the ravine. Not Sioux, not soldiers, rather fifteen Arikara braves, painted and armed for war. Although the reservation system spread far to the west, Rebecca had time to consider, the presence of these vicious killers argued well for the adage that when government was involved, some were indeed more equal than others. The Arikara were traditional enemies of the Sioux and Cheyenne. It now became obvious the army made no effort to confine them close to home, dependent on the handouts of the agency.

They seemed free to roam at will and prey upon the helpless inhabitants of the reservations, all with government blessing. Their hostile intent became obvious in strident war whoops and wild gesticulations. The leaders broke into a gallop, bringing along the warriors in a sweeping attack on the exposed couple. Rebecca had already halted the wagon and tied off the reins. She climbed down and hurried to the tail gate where she freed Sila and swung into the saddle. Her brace of Smith & Wesson No. 4 Americans comforted her. Trotting to the front of the cart, she slapped the horses into a run. Then she and Whirlwind followed the only choice they had.

Quirting their mounts, they ran. Swiftly the Arikara closed. Arrows hummed death songs in the air. A spent one clattered off Rebecca's saddle skirt. She drummed heels into Sila's flanks, drew a .44 Smith American and turned slightly to fire to the rear.

Smoke from the first shot obscured her view. She had little hope of hitting anything with a degree of accuracy. Even so, it should slow them down. Beside her, Whirlwind grunted harshly and clasped at an arrow shaft that protruded from the loose flesh of his right side. It had gone clean through, she noted with relief. Quickly she fired three more times at the closest enemies, while Whirlwind snapped off the finely honed steel point and withdrew the projectile from his side. Rebecca fired again. An Arikara warrior screamed and threw up his hands.

Wobbling erratically, he carried on with his mount a few running strides, then fell solidly to the earth. Rebecca holstered the emptied Smith, and drew the other. Whirlwind gritted teeth against the persistent ache in his side, slid the Remington from his saddle scabbard and punched a round into the heaving chest of a pursuing Arikara pony.

Squealing, the animal went down, hurtling its rider forward, to slam head-first into the ground. Only the furious thunder of pounding hoofs hid the dry stick crack of his broken neck. Slowly the distance between the two parties widened. Ahead lay the South Fork of the White River. Beyond it, the uncertain sanctuary of the Rosebud Agency. Another five hundred yards.

"Come on," Rebecca urged. "Keep going."

"I don't like any of this," Roger Styles said heatedly. He thrust back in the high-backed, horsehair-stuffed leather chair and slapped a hand on the flat table. Soft feminine chatter came from several other rooms of the huge *hacienda*, as the staff cleaned and dusted. Seated across from him, Pedro Ordaz lifted the delicate, stemmed crystal glass and sipped of the heady, per-fumed port wine. The *Tipo Ofino* had been shipped directly from Xerez in Spain to the cellar of the former owner of Las Piedras. He licked his lips and shrugged expansively. It caused his belly to shake. Too much of living the good life had taken its toll on him.

"I cautioned you about that callous murder of the boy, Don Roger," Ordaz said lightly. "Few of these locals would find that amusing, as you and my troops did. We are . . . hardened men, indifferent to death and suffering. Such a spectacle heated our blood. I, myself, visited three of the young women that night. I exploded like thunder of the Olmec rain god inside them. Twice each. No doubt you enjoyed similar re-lease. But these peons listen too much to Padre Luis. And to such over-educated, refined weaklings as our Lieutenant Alvarado." Ordaz's face clouded with anger. "Also to his father, Don Esteban Alvarado y Polanski. Did you know the old man owns a *ganadéria* that neigh-bors on mi—er, yours?"

"No I didn't," Roger responded. He swiftly drank off the port and poured another portion. "Is that of importance?"

"It is said among the villagers that Don Estebán gives sanctuary to those who oppose *Presidente* Diáz, the railroad cartel and my military governorship. What a pity. It might become necessary to have the son arrest the father for treason, and in turn to arrest the younger on the same charge."

"Ha!" Roger uttered a sharp bark of laughter and clapped his hands together. "And all this while I've believed that only the Oriental mind had the capacity for true irony and subterfuge."

"You flatter me, Excellency. Nonetheless, the fact remains that there is a conspiracy afoot. Organized resistance is developing and the first strains of rebellion are singing in the hearts of the common people. They ring also in the breast of that fool Alvarado. You can mark my words on that."

Dodge City proved a fortuitous stop. Seated at a table, like the advance man for a circus selling tickets, Chris Starret quickly filled out the four vacancies in his unholy twelve. In celebration, he delved into the ample expense money Roger Styles provided and obtained river boat and rail transportation for them all. A holiday mood still enraptured the malicious dozen when they arrived in Pierre, Dakota Territory. There, the first man they encountered was Thomas Hayden, American manager of Sir Hubert Grimsley's Dakota cattle empire.

"It's about time you got here," Hayden snapped. "Sir Hubert is about to bust open. He's written he wants results or he'll come over here from England. Get your gear and put it in the wagon out front of the depot."

"I think you've got the wrong men," Chris Starret informed the officious manager.

"No I don't. I sent for you to run those goddamned squatters out of Sir Hubert's land. You've taken far too long to get here. Time's wasting."

"We have a communications problem, it seems," Chris spoke steadily, containing his rising temper. "We were not *summoned* here by anyone. We were *sent* here. We are working for the interests of a gentleman in Mexico."

Hayden eyed him shrewdly. "Are you trying to hold us up for more money?"

"Why would I do that, when I don't even know your name?" Chris rumbled alarmingly.

Eyes blinking rapidly, the head jerking as though palsied, Hayden responded bemusedly. "It's Tom Hayden, of course. Aren—aren't you Ben Meecham?"

"Certainly not. I killed Ben Meecham three weeks ago, outside a Nogales, Sonora cantina."

"Y—you did? Why did you do that?" Hayden stammered. The contracting for violence, to be committed elsewhere, by others, had no effect on him. Direct, and personal, confrontation with it upset Hayden considerably.

"He was trying to recruit some of my boys," Chris told the middle-sized, curly-haired dude.

"Wh-who are you?" Hayden managed, sounding like an owl.

"Chris Starret."

"Oh . . . *shit*. And you killed Meecham? After I'd sent him five thousand dollars to gather a force of range detectives to oust the squatters. Wh-what did he do with the money?"

"I haven't the slightest idea," Chris told him calmly.

"But you . . . must know something. Sir Hubert will be furious," Hayden blurted.

"*Sir* Hubert can sit on a donkey hard on, for all I care," Chris suggested nastily. "It's not my problem."

"Oh, but it is. You chose to, ah, terminate him before he could fulfill his commission to us. Some sort of recompense must be made."

"You sound like some sissy New York clerk," Luke Nelson growled.

Hayden batted his nervous eyelids at him. Had he so badly misjudged this man who looked so obviously an upright and fair-minded person? "Surely, sir, you must see the undebatable gem of logic in what I'm saying?"

Luke grinned softly, like everyone's square-jawed, open-faced father. "What I see is a bugger-ass sissy trying to get us to do a dangerous job for nothing."

"Now, see here!" a brief flare of pique heated Hayden's chilled mind.

"Luke's right, Mister Hayden," Chris intervened. "I'm a reasonable man. Let's us suppose we happen to be at liberty to undertake this commission? What is this job, and what will Sir Hubert be willing to pay to have it done?"

"We've already advanced five thou—"

"Not to us, you didn't," Chris cut him off.

"Er-ah, well, then, Sir Hubert mentioned a sum of three thousand." Hayden cleared his throat. "There are eight squatter farms, at three thousand each to see them abandoned and burned down. That makes twenty-four thousand dollars, plus the expenses advanced, which we shall provide to you, if you accept the contract."

Sunbeams danced in Chris' smile. "Now those are some impressive figures."

"Sir Hubert is a generous man. But he expects a thorough and competent job to be done."

"I'm not finished yet. You mean this *foreigner* has that kind of money? He can buy up all that land, stock it with cattle, then pay thousands of dollars to have Americans run off other Americans who want to live there?"

"That, ah, sums it up rather nicely, yes," Hayden said primly.

"Don't that beat all," Hank Bridger injected. "Boys, we're in the wrong business. This bein' a Sir Somebody or other has sure got the rest beat."

"Then you're willing to do it?" Hayden urged, sensing the time to close.

"If it can be done in a week," Chris bargained.

"Oh, I'm sure, using your ingenuity, Mr. Starret, that it can be accomplished in that time," Hayden said oilily.

"Then, to clinch the deal, Mr. Hayden, you can stake us to a meal. We've had nothing but ship's food for the past nine hundred miles. A large steak, potatoes and greens, with a few good glasses of beer will do wonders."

Chapter 9

Soft, haunting music came from two Sioux flutes. A love-sick swain from the Fox clan serenaded his sweetheart, a lush girl of the Earth Lodge clan. A young husband, lonesome for his bride of three moons, also played an eerie tune of longing. It would be two more days before she returned from the *isnatipi*. The mingling of their notes, with the muted laughter of sleepy children, lazy quarrels of the dogs, and far off call of a loon, created a nostalgic mood in the village of the Red Top Lodge Oglala.

Many men had taken their backrests and blankets outside, to listen, smoke and relax in memory under the stars. Not so, Whirlwind. Still feverish from the arrow wound, he lay in the lodge, staring at a small triangle of starry sky as seen through the smoke hole. Rebecca sat at his side, quiet, intent on nursing him. She also felt certain she would hear again of the repeating rifle.

They had lost the entire wagonload, the mules and vehicle. She had received an irritating, painful bullet scrape along the outside of her left thigh. With Whirlwind's two wounds, and the utter indifference of the Agency authorities to do anything about the unpro-

voked attack, she considered it more than ample reason to resurrect the line of logic which said a seven shot
repeater in Whirlwind's hands, as well as her own
fifteen shooter in hers would have given them a chance
to save their two weeks of hard work. Conscious now,
Whirlwind's eyes had, in her imagination, an accusing
look.

"Mother." Joey's sudden entrance distracted Rebecca
from her concerns. "We're going hunting early in the
morning. May I stay with *Kehala?*"

"Yes, *Pinzpinzala*. What time do you leave?" Rebecca
asked.

"Before Sun Boy comes. Ah . . . about three in the
morning," Joey added in English.

The boy had been finding it difficult to think in his
native language of late and Rebecca encouraged him to
use it when they were in private. Recently she had
come to the conclusion that they could not spend the
rest of their lives here with the Oglala. Joey needed
schooling. She needed some purpose beyond daily living. No matter the relationships they formed here,
when that time came they would have to be able to
adjust to a white world again. Still bound by the
present, though, she rose and moved to where she
stored the food supplies.

"Take these dough cakes with you, then. They're
sweetened with honey and will provide breakfast without building a fire that might scare off game."

Joey beamed. "Thank you, mother. Without them
we would have had to do with parched corn and some
buffalo jerky." Taking up his rifle and cartridges, sling-
ing hunting bow, quiver of arrows and sheath knife, the
slender, leggy youth stopped at the entrance flap. "We'll
be gone, ah, two days."

"Jo—!" Rebecca started to protest. Resignedly she
amended her words. "Bring me back at least an ante-

93

lope."

A hundred rainbows, sparked by the sun through prismatic glass in the upper half of the tall, narrow windows, danced in the great hall of the *hacienda*. Seated at a long, sturdy table, Estebán Alvarado y Polanski glowered at the stack of expense reports his *mayorál* had placed before him half an hour earlier. Outside the verdant magic of a San Luis Potósi springtime went unnoticed by the aging *ganádero*.

"Political double talk and nonsense," Don Estebán said aloud to no one. " 'It is for the benefit of the landholders,' " he quoted sarcastically. "I have never heard of this policy of 'nationalizing' something. What does it mean?"

Three men entered, greeting the *ganádero* affably. They removed riding capes and hats and took chairs. Don Estebán summoned a servant and sent him for refreshments. Then he returned to the topic of his resentment.

"*Nationalize*. It's a word without a meaning. Do we know that this is a program from the government in Mexico? So far, the only one who seems to benefit from it is our military governor. With the railroad in the hands of the government, this Captain Mendoza charges us four times the former rate to ship bulls, or any produce to market. All, except Ordaz and his *succubus* from *la Capitál*, *Señor* Styles. Which brings me to why I asked you here."

"Yes, Don Estebán, we are all curious," a prosperous strawberry farmer from south of the bull ranches urged. "What do you have in mind?"

"This *Señor* Styles seems to have a great deal of money. The crushing railroad freight charges are hurting many. Are you aware that more than twenty local

94

business men and *haciendados* alike have been forced to grant the *gringo* half interest in their enterprises in order to stay in business?"

"Is it that bad, Don Estebán?" Hector Marávillas asked.

"Only too true," Alvarado assured him. "And the rest of us are rapidly going broke. We face a terrible crisis and nothing, it seems, can be done about it."

"Even the railroad people are unhappy," David Récendes observed. "They say that none of the other lines have been seized by the government. Did you know, Don Estebán, that the workers are worse off than before? Although they are being paid more, they work longer hours and there is no repair work being done on the track. It's becoming dangerous. If they wish to leave their jobs, they are told that they do so at the forfeit of their lives."

Estebán Alvarado frowned pensively. "Then I have acted wisely. I called you here to inform you that I have appealed to men in the National Assembly whom I consider to be most reliable. I have asked that the government in *la Capítal* conduct an investigation."

"That is risky," Hector Marávillas complained. "Coronel Ordaz and the *gringo*, Styles, have the ear of the *presidente*."

"We cannot sit here and do nothing," Don Estebán countered. "Also, my son tells me there is growing unrest on Las Piedras. It may be only the usual peon grumbling. I want nothing to do with a peasant uprising. Such things tend to spread and the precedent is dangerous. On the other hand, if they have just grievances, perhaps it could work to our advantage. If any of you have something to contribute, that would also help. We're facing disaster and ruin, *Señores*, at least we should face it like men . . . and fight for what we have."

Blazing nicely, the nearly completed barn gave off quite human shrieks and moans as it collapsed in on itself and sent up a huge shower of sparks. Four of the masked "range detectives" methodically shot panicked cattle in a corral. Under a large pine, a sobbing woman, dressed in a nightgown, leaned against her husband. He wore a nightshirt and, like his wife and children, was barefoot. In a low monotone, he ineffectually cursed these men who had come in the night.

Thadeus Greene had heard of others being rousted from their homesteads by the so-called detectives. It couldn't happen to him, he believed. He had filed all proper and legal. When the knock had come at midnight, with the order for he and his wife and children to get out, he had told the leader so.

"Makes no difference. This is open range. You can't go filing on that," the gruff voice had told him. "You've got five minutes. Then we set this place afire."

The leader sat his horse a short distance from Thad and his wife now. He removed his hat to wipe perspiration from his brow. Firelight reflected orangely from his bald head. Thad wished for his shotgun. A tug at his nightshirt sleeve brought his attention to his eight year old son.

"What is it, Lane?"

"When are the bad men going, Poppa?"

"I don't know, son."

"They said we have to leave here. But they've killed old Bessie an' her calf. Shootin' the horses, too. How are we going to go?"

"We'll walk, I suppose, Lane. Now you care for your sister, hear?"

"Yes, sir."

"That's enough, boys," the leader called out in his strangely accented voice. "I think Mister Greene understands now."

"Sure enough, Chris," Hank Bridger answered. "There's a buckboard and four horses around back we saved for them."

"That's mighty considerate of you, Hank. Make sure Mister Greene thanks you properly for that," Chris responded sarcastically. "We're through here, Mister Greene," he addressed the farmer.

"You've ruined me," Thad Greene mustered spunk enough to complain. "You're nothing but common brigands."

"That may be, Mr. Greene. But we consider it a form of range justice," Chris told him mildly. "Your neighbor, Edwards, is going to get a taste of it next."

Slipping through the trees with as little sound as a mountain cat, Jose Archuleta left the meeting place hurriedly. The moon had long since set and frosty stars provided minimal light to negotiate the treacherous mountain slopes. Far below, on the road, he had left his burro at a small, noisy, and incredibly dirty tavern. Archuleta had better than a mile to go. He wouldn't dare stay the night.

Arriving at Las Piedras the next day would arouse more suspicion than his absence tonight. It had gone well. Others felt the same as he. Those who suffered more than any under this new military governorship were the small merchants. Jose owned the *mercado* in San Simon de Guanera, one of the villages on Las Piedras. Although the *Patrón* apparently did not suffer from the new taxes and high freight prices, he surely did. Tins of fish, fruit and chilis, barrels of sugar, vinegar, jars of olive oil all came by rail and now cost three times their previous price. His customers could not afford to pay and he couldn't either. It was the same everywhere.

Angry merchants and ranch foremen met in this secret place. They had decided, among other things, to make Jose one of the leaders. What exactly they would do had not been agreed upon. All the same, they were organized now and plans could be made. The peons groaned under new work loads. Perhaps they could form some sort of mutual force to oppose this unfair treatment? Distance dissolved in contemplation and Jose stopped himself before breaking out of the woods onto the open roadway.

Cautiously he peered about, looking up and down the narrow, white slash of rutted path. At last he satisfied himself that he was alone. Jose stepped out on the road and started off with a jaunty stride. Far off, at the opposite end of a large curve, he saw the tiny yellow wink of a tavern lamp. He'd be there with time to spare, Jose estimated.

"*Alto! Los manós arriba*," the deep voice came from the trees. Its meaning, though, left no doubt.

To Jose's right, the woods, and obviously a pair of mounted figures. To his left, a sheer dropoff of a thousand feet. Gulping back his fear, Jose Archuleta stopped and raised his hands.

"Let's go check our prize, Sergeant," a younger, lighter voice spoke in the darkness.

Jose watched with the resignation of a trapped animal while a young officer and a thin, sharp-eyed sergeant walked their horses onto the trail. At a distance of twenty paces, they dismounted and dropped their reins. Starshine glinted off the barrel of a revolver in the hand of the officer. Jose cringed inwardly. The thought of a bullet tearing into his flesh seemed too horrible to contemplate.

"Ummm. A familiar face, no? What do you think, Alvarez? Is this not Jose Archuleta from San Simon del

Guanera? The grocer?"

"You know me, *Teniente*," Jose responded in a surly tone, some of his valor recovered. "Do not toy with me."

"What are you doing here, Archuleta?" Lt. Alvarado demanded.

"I wished to get away from my store and my family for a while," Jose told him, not altogether untruthfully.

"A long way to go. Man, you're more than half way to Guanájuato. There are bandits in these mountains."

"So I have been told," Jose acknowledged. "Some of them, no doubt at the tavern where I left my burro. That's why I'm in a hurry to get back there. I don't want him stolen."

"It's a shame that the sergeant and I are alone. We might get some reward money for raiding that place, eh, Paco?"

"Or we might get our *cójones* cut off, Lieutenant," the ever-practical Alvarez suggested. "How many of your other merchant friends felt the need to escape their families tonight, Archuleta?" the short, thin, intense non-com asked sharply, revealing their knowledge of the secret gathering.

"Why, ah, why, none. I am, as you can see . . . alone," Jose evaded hopefully.

"That may be true . . . for the moment," Alvarado allowed. "The rest of my patrol is combing these mountains. They might catch some other, surprising fish, *como no?*"

Anguish and the injustice of his situation twisted Jose's face into a mask of wretchedness. "*Teniente*, this is an outrage. All of it. Your father is a *haciendado*. He suffers like I do, like those who live on his land do. Only a chosen few are safe from the new taxes, the high prices, the arrogance of *Coronel* Ordaz. I have said enough to be put against the wall. I don't care any

99

more. You are a man of conscience, *Señor* Alvarado. A man of education and culture. You are your father's son. How can you countenance serving such a master in light of the suffering it is causing your friends, your neighbors, your family?"

A long silence followed Jose's impassioned plea. For a moment he thought he would break out with a despairing sob. Then young Alvarado stepped forward and placed a hand on his shoulder.

"Look up at me, Jose Archuleta," the youthful officer said in a tone of softness and regret, which grew as he spoke with great feeling. "Your secret is safe with us. I do not countenance what is going on. My heart has ached since the unspeakable murder of that child at the *tienta*. I have shame for the uniform I wear, where once I knew nothing but unquenchable pride. Alvarez is with me in this. So are my men. They are, ah, not patrolling the mountainsides. They're searching the interior of the beer barrel and tequila bottles at that tavern you mentioned. No one will be caught tonight. No names added to a list.

"But you must keep this a secret, Jose Archuleta. On the soul of your mother. No one is to know of our sentiments. Keep no lists yourselves. When the time is right, we will be there to help. Come, put a leg up behind Alvarez and we'll take you to within a short walk of the tavern. Then I shall call out my troops and we will return to our outpost. When the way is clear, *vaya con díos*, Jose Archuleta."

With the last squatter fled to other parts, and the last odor of burning hay clear of their nostrils, the band of hardcases led by Chris Starret returned to Pierre and settled down to their primary mission. Through feelers Chris had put out prior to their eight day excursion into running off homesteaders, he had garnered considerable information about the half-breed girl known as Rebecca Caldwell Ridgeway.

Much of it was useless, as he had suspected. One item, verified by three separate sources, caught his attention. To the best of anyone's knowledge, Rebecca Caldwell Ridgeway now resided with the Oglala half of her bloodline, on the Rosebud Reservation.

"Look at this, boys. Here's a tintype picture of the one we're after. In this Territory newspaper. That's when she was gettin' hitched to a feller named Grover Ridgeway. Good looker, isn't she?"

"Ummm. I wouldn't throw rocks at her," Luke Nelson observed.

"*Séguro*," Harry Gonzáles-Gonzáles agreed. "An' I know something I'd like to throw in her."

"We're here," Chris reminded them, "to bring the lady back to Mexico. Unharmed if possible."

"Do you think it'll work out that way, Boss?" Jerry Tibbs asked trustingly.

"That depends a great deal on the lady," Chris told him.

Chapter 10

Angry shouts sent the swallows fluttering nervously from their nests among the tiles of the *hacienda* roof. Several peons, walking past on their way to the bean fields to hoe weeds, paused and crossed themselves. The words echoed off the plastered front wall of the church, across the small, fountain-adorned square from the *hacienda*.

"*Are you certain?*" Clearly the voice of Don Estebán Alvarado y Polanski.

The answer, unheard by those outside, came in a hushed tone.

"*¡Condenácion!* Is there no end to the corruption and dishonor during the reign of this . . . this *bufón* Díaz? At every turn we are at the mercy of grasping criminals. *¡Jésus, Mária y Jóse!* Is there not one man, *one man* whom we can trust?"

The same four had gathered, this time in Don Estebán's study. Hector Marávillas leaned forward, brow furrowed with worry as Don Estebán and a clean cut looking young man stepped into the room. "What is it, Don Estebán?"

"My messenger here has brought me disastrous news, gentlemen. It appears that *Coronel* Ordaz had foreknowledge of the deputation coming from *la Capital*. He met the government emissary, a *Señor* Ephraím Enchausti, and neutralized him with threats and a big bribe. This is fact, gentlemen. There was a witness to the proceeding, a Pedro Lopez, waiter in the private car Enchausti used."

"How did it happen?" David Récendes queried.

"The train was stopped, Ordaz came aboard with two of his most intimidating associates, and they sat down with Enchausti to drink his liquor, eat his food and tell him, ah-no, make it *order* him what to do."

Hearing the last of this revelation while passing in the hall, Xavier Alvarado entered the study. "Father. Gentlemen. Good afternoon to you all. I couldn't help hearing, Father. I should have told you earlier. In light of this, it has become even more important. The merchants here in Guanájuato, and in Nayarít, have become angry at Ordaz, also. They are banding together in an organization to fight this oppression. I know one of their leaders. Perhaps together you can exert enough influence in the capital to force change."

Esteban Alvarado shook his head. "Only if there was enough time. That, I'm afraid, is not possible. With this betrayal, I am certain that I shall soon become the next victim of confiscation and taxation."

"We must fight, Father," Xavier urged.

"Who?"

"You, our people, my Lancers, the people of the other ranches and *fincas*."

"And who, pray tell, shall supply the inspiring, uniting leadership?"

Xavier's face fell. "I . . . at this time, I . . . don't know."

103

Definitely on the way to sound recovery, Whirlwind chafed at his imposed inactivity. Rebecca still waited for the thunderclap of his discontent over the rifle. He had so far refrained from all but censorious looks and silent hostility. In hopes of generating a more pleasant mood, she arranged for a picnic to their secret spot at the falls. To her relief, Whirlwind responded eagerly. With provisions tied behind them, they rode out from the Oglala village shortly after sunrise. At the usual spot, they left the horses hobbled and proceeded on foot. The day seemed light and carefree. They had not even taken any precautions about riding directly to their goal.

Such lightheartedness suited Anse Angleton. Chris Starret and his hardcases had established a hidden camp some miles from where the Red Top Lodge band had set up their camp. They had drawn lots to keep the village under observation. Today's four hour morning watch had fallen to Anse. Careful planning made the operation near to foolproof. The last watch of the day was not relieved until a man came out to make sure he had not been led away. That allowed the stalker on duty to follow with the assurance the gang would eventually be right behind. Anse had hardly taken position when the picnickers departed.

Angleton hastily fashioned a trail pointer and set off in pursuit. When he came upon the abandoned horses, it took Anse a while to determine what had happened. After diligently quartering the ground, he discovered the little game trail and noted human footprints on it. He ground-reined his mount and started off after the elusive couple.

Rebecca and Whirlwind reached the small, grassy

104

glade. There they spread a blanket and set aside their buckskin bags of carefully prepared food. Each unwilling to break the mood they had created, they stood silent for a moment, like shy children. Then Rebecca knelt and removed her moccasins. She rose gracefully, unaware that unseen, startled eyes took in their every action. With an easy, practiced movement, she pulled off her dress.

Anse Angleton thought he might choke on the gasp he fought to contain. Oh, Lordy, what a body. His eyes burned and his mouth went dry. The small, firmly upthrust breasts seemed to call out to him. Narrow waist, flaring hips, well rounded thighs. He felt himself rapidly stiffen and groped beneath his belt to relieve the strain.

"We can't go swimming," Rebecca said simply. "Or do anything else with clothes on."

"I might be too weak for swimming," Whirlwind responded. "But the 'or something' sounds good."

Excitement charged Rebecca. It would be the first time since before the disastrous encounter with the Arikara. Avidly she watched while Whirlwind removed his clothing. Rebecca moaned at the sight of his engorged shaft and sank to her knees. She took him with both hands and stroked urgently.

Whirlwind shuddered and, along with him, Anse. The hidden voyeur could not ignore the pain radiating from his loins. He loosened his trousers and began to ease himself with a slow, irregular motion. Rebecca's lips closed over Whirlwind's maleness. Anse thought he would go wild. It reminded him of the time when he was eleven. He had finally worked up nerve to spy on his older sister and her beau through the peep hole he had made in the wall.

It had started in a flurry of petticoats and bedlinen. Then the action had gotten started. At first, little Anse could not believe his own sister would touch a man's flesh. The way she stroked it soon convinced Anse he wasn't the only one in the Angleton family to have experience. When his sister sat on the bed and Buster Norton knelt in front of her, Anse nearly gagged. Buster actually buried his head between her legs and began to lick her.

At his tender age, Anse considered *that* revolting. But he still had his pecker in his hand, yanking away for all his might, eye fixed tightly to his spy hole. After that, things happened fast. And kept on happening. By the time the amorous pair had satisfied their lusts, Anse had spilled his vital syrup against his bedroom wall three times. He'd had to hurry to clean up the mess. And now . . . oh, Lordy, this coppery beauty had taken nearly all of that redskin in while he day-dreamed. While Anse stared, enraptured, Whirlwind churned his hips in a frenzy.

Rebecca worked with consummate skill to draw the most in pleasure for them both. Time whirled around them and all but the eternal now mattered. Before his ultimate eruption, Rebecca flung herself backward and cried out to him.

"Now, Whirlwind. Oh, hurry beloved. Pierce me to my heart."

For his part, Whirlwind tried.

Urgently they spent themselves, rekindled their passion and engaged in raptures beyond all ken until the sun passed far over the middle of the sky. Weak with their exertions, drained of long-suppressed stamina, they walked dazedly to the stream and entered. Rebecca bathed languidly, luxuriating in the chill of the water and the contrasting warm vibrations of her well-satisfied body. Whirlwind floundered about like a joyful porpoise. Refreshed, they climbed out.

"Let's dry off on that rock," Rebecca suggested, as usual, speaking in Lakota. "Then we'll eat. This afternoon I want to dive for more gold."

"Why?" Whirlwind asked, frowning. "We've no need in the village to buy more new things."

"I . . . want to buy you that Winchester. Right or wrong, I should have allowed you to make your choice. I don't want . . . something like that to come between us."

Whirlwind laughed loudly. "And here . . . here I . . . I've been absolutely thundering mad at myself for not finding the words to tell you it didn't matter. Oh, *Sinaskawin*, what a pair we are."

The words meant nothing to Anse Angleton. But the sights he had seen had worked their erotic effect on his over-charged body. Like the horny lad of his past, he had several times wetly expended himself on the grass. He'd only tidied up when he felt a touch on his boot heel. He turned swiftly and saw Chris peering at him.

"She's there," Anse whispered close to Chris' ear. "I just watched her fuck a big Sioux buck cross-eyed. Man, has she got a body!"

"Ah-ha. Let's go get her then," Chris suggested with a winsome smile.

Still naked, Rebecca knelt over the first bag, opening it to take out two coal-roasted prairie hens and some cornmeal frybread. She looked up at the sound of a snapping twig. Whirlwind's long, handsome body did not fill her gaze. She saw instead three fully dressed, hard-faced white men moving rapidly toward her.

"Look out!" she cried, looking around to find them

both surrounded by a dozen leering gunmen.

Whirlwind dived for his rifle. He clutched at it, rolled and came up. A moment later, the heavy barrel of a seven inch Colt .45 slammed into his forehead. He went over backward, limbs twitching uncontrollably. Rebecca bit off a scream and tried to run toward her sixguns. A grinning bulk of a man cut her off.

"You done knocked that one into the next world," Jerry Tibbs remarked to Wes Davidson.

"Yer right, Kid," Wes agreed. "He's sure twitchin' like's he's a goner."

"What are you doing here?" Rebecca demanded in English, finding her voice again. "You're on the reservation."

"We care quite little about the reservation," Chris told her. "And to answer your question, we've come to get you, Missy Rebecca."

They knew her name. Rebecca chilled at the realization. "You can't hope to get away with it. There are soldiers out, the Indian Police, hunting parties from our band and the others," Rebecca tried to argue for her freedom.

"We got here, didn't we?" Kid Tibbs smirked.

"You shoulda been here earlier, Kid," Anse chortled. "She an' that buck were making the beast with two backs. She sure can do it. He's hung like a stud donkey. She'd go astraddle of it an' took him all in. I thought she was like to split herself open. They got to churnin' around like a piston on one of them big ol' steam locomotives. Her titties were a jigglin' and she made those little ol' sounds. Like to drive a feller crazy watchin'."

"Was it real excitin'?" the Kid asked avidly. His own experience in amorous endeavors had been limited to some cuddling and mutual masturbation, and one hurried and unfulfilling roll in the hay with a girl four years younger than he.

"You know it Kid. And they did other things to each other such as you've never dreamed of before."

"Tell me," the Kid urged.

"We'd best get her away from here quick," Harry Gonzales-Gonzales suggested.

Anse and the Kid wandered off a way. Anse made graphic gestures as he explained to the baby-faced gunman all the intimate details of the tender love scene he had spied upon. The Kid's face flushed and he groped at his crotch as the conversation continued.

"Where are you taking me? Why?"

"Man wants to see you real bad," Chris replied helpfully. "Down Mexico way. Does the name Roger Styles mean anything to you?"

Chapter 11

Like all men who lived by the saddle, Chris Starret's gunfighters felt vulnerable separated by nearly a quarter mile from their horses. Harry Gonzales-Gonzales' suggestion was acted upon with alacrity. One of the gang grabbed up Rebecca's dress and moccasins and they started off to where their mounts waited. Although fired by lust from Anse Angleton's vivid oratory, the hungry looks in their eyes warning Rebecca of the inevitable, they refrained from assaulting her there at the stream, or later when they regained their horses. Chris studied his men as they milled about, minds half made up to satisfy their aroused passions immediately.

"We have to be well away from the reservation come sundown," Chris advised. "Someone is bound to miss those two and come looking. Whatever you have in mind can wait until then."

"Aw, Chris, we ain't been close to a woman in . . ." Anse Angleton protested.

"You won't be for a while, either," Chris interrupted. "Mount up and let's ride."

Chris allowed Rebecca to take her own horse, the palouse stallion, Sila. Although her wrists had been shackled in front of her and a short length of rope hung between her ankles under Sila's belly, Rebecca had some limited choice of where she rode in the outlaw pack. Believing Whirlwind to be dead, and knowing eventual rape was inevitable, she decided to single out the obvious leader, the one the men called Chris, and gain his protection. She cantered up beside him and tried for conversation.

"Roger Styles isn't noted for his generosity toward underlings," Rebecca opened her campaign. "Matter of fact, he's been known to kill someone, even when they did a perfect job, rather than pay them."

Chris chuckled "I'm quite sure he knows better than to try that with me. Tell me, what is it between you and Roger?"

Rebecca tried a coaxing smile. "I am one of several persons who broke up Roger's great plans in this country and forced him into exile in Mexico."

"Exile is it? It must suit him well. He's rich and powerful, has a huge *rancho*, a *ganadería* actually, on the border between the states of San Luis Potósi and Guanájuato. And he has the ear of *Presidente* Diáz."

"Roger always was an oily customer. He could worm his way into the confidence of anyone, as long as they had a goodly streak of corruption in them. But he's no real man." Rebecca lowered long, black lashes over her deep blue eyes, blatantly flirting with the outlaw leader. "I could be very accommodating and affectionate for a real, strong man who would look out for my wellbeing."

Once more Chris laughed, this time with a nasty edge to the guffaws. "Ah, woman, the eternal conniver. Wasn't it Eve who got Adam to bite the apple?" He chuckled again. "Nice try. But as far as I'm concerned, you're community property all the way to Roger's *haci-*

enda way down in *mañana* land. After all, any slut who would lie with a red nigger should be pleased to have eleven whites and a Mexican trifle with her."

Stung, Rebecca kept her temper. "I'm certain that you are aware I am half, ah, red nigger," she said tartly. "If you're so afraid of contamination by association with one, perhaps I have nothing to worry about at all."

"I'm sure the boys will be glad to pretend your sepia color is in the half they're not using at the time. As for myself, you've made your point. Although you are a certain beauty, I shall refrain."

Ice coated Rebecca's heart. She had set out to gain his protection, and in the process endure his rutting to insure it. All she had accomplished had been to neutralize him. Now she could only look forward to the worst possible outcome.

Big Nose had been out hunting since early morning. Pride and confidence filled him with the comfortable weight of the new Remington rifle. He had started off certain of bringing in some tasty game. That had been before he encountered the odd trail. One of the three horses that had made the fresh sign he recognized as Whirlwind's, from the familiar imprint in soft ground. He had followed a short distance and saw where Becky's stallion had urinated, the splash marks bored a neat hole in the center of the damp spot. Then he came upon a place where the third rider had deliberately delayed his fidgeting animal in a hidden depression.

With that evidence, Big Nose had correctly assumed that his friends were being stalked. By a white man, the iron shoe marks of the third pony revealed. He had pressed on, until he suddenly saw a group of eleven rough-looking riders quartering cross-country and studying the ground as they cantered along on an intersecting route. Big Nose dropped off his pony and caused it to lie down.

When the strange white men hit the trail, they let out a whoop and began to follow it like a pack of hunting wolves. Big Nose knew his friends were in bad trouble. If he rode back to camp for help, he would be too late to aid them. Silently he had debated the alternatives. He had concluded that on the off chance someone would see the smoke and remember the sequence, he could send a smoke signal for help, then follow the hunters, or try to out-guess Whirlwind as to his destination, then take an alternate route.

He had opted for this course of action. After all, it had been easy. Where would Big Nose take a girl he loved? To Spirit Creek, of course. Now he branched off and took a shorter, but more rugged trail for the tiny paradise.

Rebecca gathered her strayed and unproductive thoughts. Her first priority had to be finding a way to escape. After much internal debate, she decided to try to lull the bandits into becoming careless. Given their present frame of mind, to do that she must convince them she wanted, and enjoyed, their sexual advances. And to do that, she'd have to first convince herself. In an effort to prepare herself, she started to respond to their lewd comments.

"I don't cotton to a sunburned rump, Sister, so you got a while," Luke Nelson assured her.

"Wait until moonrise, and I'll show you something you never expected," Rebecca taunted.

"That Injun might have been hung like a prize stud, Missy," Anse Angleton snickered, "but I'll tell you somethin'. You ain't never had anything until you have Anse Angleton."

"When I do, I still won't have had anything," Rebecca quipped saucily.

"How about me, Anse? Huh—huh?" Jerry Tibbs bubbled. "They say these white squaws got a real hanker for young, white pecker."

"That depends on whether I can find it or not," Rebecca wise-cracked. Then she feigned a serious-sensual expression. "Truth is, I like all you boys. *Any* boys, for that matter, no matter their size. Long ones, short ones, thick ones, thin ones, crooked ones, ones with warts on the tip . . . yep, I love 'em all." To her utter surprise, Rebecca found herself actually getting aroused by this talk. Her heart pounded and her loins grew warm.

"Oh, yes, we're gonna have a fine time," she went on. "I can't wait to make camp and share the sunset with one of you lucky fellows."

"I can't wait, either," Jerry Tibbs squeaked in a breaking voice. "I think I'm gonna split my pecker skin."

"Not until *afterward*, little guy. You were right about us squaws liking young, white . . ." She almost choked on the word, "pecker."

"Yeeeowwwwiieee!" Kid Tibbs wailed.

"The point, is," Chris growled, "you'll all wait." In a softer voice, close to Rebecca's ear, he went on. "I don't entirely buy your act, Miss Rebecca Caldwell. Of a

114

sudden, you seem too eager."

Rebecca chilled a moment, then a flash of sensual stimulation washed over her. "Truth is, I'm getting terribly eager."

The small cavalcade had covered a good thirty-five miles from the reservation when Chris called a halt a bit before sunset. Camp took shape quickly, while the hardcases gave Rebecca bold glances. When Chris gauged he could contain them no longer, he gave the go-ahead.

"Me first?" Anse pleaded. "I've been achin' long enough. Longer than anybody."

"Go on, Anse," Chris declared. "Only don't blame me if she scratches out your eyes."

Anse Angleton proved to have a short, quick fuse and a faulty powder charge. Following his uninspired, rabbit-like thumping, the lineup began in earnest. Rebecca steeled her mind to what she must do and to the mortification she would otherwise feel at such a procession of males, rutting out of anger more than lust. By the time it became the turn of Kid Tibbs, who had grown wildly over-stimulated, Rebecca had overcome her revulsion and participated quite freely.

"Owww, dang it," Kid Tibbs groaned when his penis popped out after only two short thrusts. He shuddered with delight when he felt *her* hand guiding him back.

One, two, three . . . *it happened again!* "What's the matter with you?" he growled, hiding his own hurt and humiliation.

"You can't sink a well with too short a drill," Rebecca answered sweetly. "Relax, I'll help you."

Her words brought snickers from the band of hardcases standing around. Face flaming, Jerry Tibbs culled up visions of that disastrous first, and only other, time. He may have been sixteen, and bigger, but it was little Sally who had been the teacher, and he the pupil. When he'd popped out for the third time, she began to giggle and make fun of him. Jerry wanted to cry. Manfully grasping his shattered composure he had tried again. They managed half a dozen strokes. Despite his avid concentration, Jerry could not match her smooth, insistent rhythm. Seven . . . eight . . . ni—. Suddenly the world lurched beneath him and Jerry's head spun away into that delightful oblivion he associated with the eruption of his sap. In the sweet aftermath, much to his horror, he discovered that in the instant before his explosion he had been ejected once more.

"What's the matter with you?" Sally had complained in a whiny voice. "That didn't last no time at all. I didn't have any fun."

Jerry had wilted rapidly. To his growing humiliation, no matter how skillful Sally had been with nimble fingers and silken lips, she remained unable to engender new life. They parted at last, with angry words. Sally's final belittling of him left an indelible brand on his tender psyche. Now he found himself no better able to perform. Particularly under the watchful, cynical eyes of the gunmen he rode with.

No, wait! Incredibly it seemed to be working. Wave after wave of the most invigorating sensations thundered through him. He'd never known such delight. Oh, keep on. Don't let it stop. His heart pounded and he churned with an awakening of unsuspected knowledge. Oh, if it could only last . . . for . . . EVER!

"Would you look at him," Jim Elkhorn drawled "Just

like a rabbit. Wham-bam, thank you ma'am."

Somehow, despite his heightened joy, Jerry knew he had failed again. Wordlessly, without even the thank you he had planned to give this wild, savage woman, he withdrew to the darkness beyond the fire. Behind him, Rebecca lay dazed. The boy's pitiful efforts had at least provided a respite from hard and degrading work. Her back hurt, the ground hard under the thin blanket. She was hungry and thirsty and disgusted. She thought far less of her plan now. Rebecca realized she had gone too far in an attempt to beguile the lusty outlaws.

She'd like to stop, but forced a cheerful expression and feigned compliance as the men came back for seconds. Rebecca had only too clear an idea of how they would beat and ravage her if she didn't continue her ill-conceived act and lost their confidence in her willing nature. Hopefully the boy would conquer his feeling of failure and come back to give her a little rest. As things stood, that looked like her only hope.

Big Nose saw the red-tailed hawk jink away from the area of the ravine where he believed Spirit Creek to be and knew his guess had been correct. If only he was in time to warn his friends. Blending from pale blue to deep cobalt, the sky created a shimmering dome, a magic backdrop against which the large, colorful bird gracefully soared. Pinion feathers spread and curving upward, it hovered in a large spiral, riding the thermals. Suddenly it uttered a barely audible *skree-skree* and dove on its helpless victim. It was much the same with a powerful warrior, Big Nose thought grimly. Or a large force set out to attack a much smaller one. If only he had time to warn his friends.

Some extra sense told him he had come too late. After determining that the dangerous-looking men he had encountered indeed followed Whirlwind and *Sinaskawin*, Big Nose had taken a circuitous route that had been shorter but much more difficult than that of the others. Now he had a thankfully short distance to cover on foot.

He left his horse when it could go no further. Coming in dead opposite the expected approach, he walked up the dry and sandy creek bed until it became moist, then running with water. Soon he slipped and slid over slick rocks as he traversed a tight tunnel of vegetation. He gained the trio of pools at the falls and had to clamber up the steep wall beside the water course since no rope extended to ease his way up the slippery granite. His growing anxiety made him want to call out, yet he repressed the urge. He realized that if he had come too late, there would be no escaping for him. He'd be shot like an animal in a trap. Finally out of the ravine, Big Nose saw no signs of anyone, in the open or hiding. He ran the short distance to the meadow, shouting his warning at last.

Perceived dimly at first, the familiar voice of Big Nose brought Whirlwind back to throbbing consciousness. A wave of nausea gripped him and he spewed up a sour bile. Objects close at hand blurred into fuzzy, indistinct shapes. Whirlwind groaned and tried to focus on the middle distance, where a moving object could be discerned. His effort set the world to spinning. Not until Big Nose reached his side could Whirlwind manage to come to his knees.

118

"Are you hurt, brother?" Big Nose asked anxiously.

"Of course I've been hurt," Whirlwind snapped, giving vent to the agony in his body. "Where is *Sinaskawin?* Where is she?"

Big Nose searched and found no sign of her, except the food hampers. He returned to find Whirlwind standing upright, his vision clearer. "There were men," Whirlwind explained. "White men."

Big Nose nodded. "I saw them from a distance. I waited and sent a signal, then came the back way. I found tracks, they must have taken her."

"Where?" the urgent question crackled in the peaceful glade.

"We will have to follow," Big Nose suggested.

"I will go after her at once. You go find her friend, the Crow medicine walker, Lone Wolf. Then catch up to me."

"You are too hurt to do this," Big Nose protested.

"Do as I say," Whirlwind growled, then started off unsteadily toward the path that led to the horses.

Chapter 12

High on a craggy bluff sat the blond-haired Crow mystic, Lone Wolf. His white man's pale skin had sunbaked to the ruddy copper color of his adopted people. Oblivious to both the beauty that surrounded him, and the dizzying heights he faced, he remained unmoving. Unfocused, his haunting gray eyes never wavered as a great golden eagle crossed less than ten feet in front and screeched annoyance. Icy winds fluttered the tufted ends of the yellow braids that lay against the hard ridges of muscle on his stomach. Of this, he was also unaware. Imperceptibly, the sun traveled across a deep blue sky toward a lowering bank of angry black clouds.

Distant thunder cannonaded through the deep gorges, and Lone Wolf at last stirred. He reached for the ornately beaded, buckskin case of his medicine pipe. With it in hand, he rose upon his crossed legs, smoothly as a cat stretching. He showed no sign of stiffness for his long vigil. Packing the pipe unhurriedly in the face of the approaching storm, he lit it and made offering of smoke to the six directions. His manner indicated a deeper inner meaning than the ritual usually conveyed.

His obeisance given, he finished the charge of tobacco, streaming a thin plume of smoke against a black curtain, alive with brilliant lightning flashes. Lone Wolf knocked the dottle from his pipe, replaced it in the case, and walked leisurely toward his camp. He had established his secular residence in a large, clean cave, wind and water eroded into the face of the mountain where he came to visit with the spirits. He entered its warm shelter as the first drops of rain began to fall.

Lips parted, he uttered a low, "Huh, huh, huh," like an inquisitive horse. A buffalo horn oil lamp lighted, he began to pack the extraneous things that had accumulated around the much-used camp site. With a delicate clicking, hoofs placed carefully, Lone Wolf's horse entered the cavern and shook off a great fan of water.

"Ho, big one," Lone Wolf called out through laughter. "Who is it that hasn't sense enough to come in out of the rain?"

At once he set aside his parfleche bags and began to rub his mount dry with handsful of sweet grass. "It's time for us to leave, old fellow," he addressed the horse. "Becky is in trouble again. She's been hurt and is a captive. We must make a long and hazardous ride to find her. Be strong, my friend, for great danger lies at the end of our journey. Even now Big Nose, of the Red Top Lodge Oglala is searching for us."

Even though she was continuously sore, Rebecca Caldwell Ridgeway found that she could be thankful for the rigors of the trail. Familiarity, and all too easy access, had caused the bandits' interest in her to fall off over the last week. The fatiguing pace set by Chris Starret often left them too tired by nightfall to even think about the services of their sexual toy. So much so that for the past two nights, she had only been required to submit and feign pleasure for four of the hardcases each evening. As they rode into the late afternoon, she learned from Chris a different reason in the relaxation of her amorous duties.

"It's not so much any concern I have over your condition, Miss Caldwell. I have an obligation to my employer, and to myself, to see that you are indeed delivered to Las Piedras. To insure that, I've set up a rotating schedule for the men, so that you have less chance of winning over one of them and effecting an escape."

Disappointment flooded her. "I . . . see. At least it lets me get a little rest, and I'm grateful for that."

What could she do now? It seemed the bastard could read her mind. She still had one slim chance. Through the long days, and lustful nights, Rebecca had by her lights been making some headway with the youngest of the gang. Unfortunately he was also the least experienced and lethal of them. Kid Tibbs, Jerry, Rebecca recalled his first name, had come to actually believe that she preferred him to the others. Fact was, she had to admit, she did favor him over the unwashed brutes who hungered after her more to humiliate her than to relieve their passions.

Jerry's tender, almost timid, manner of lovemaking never left her sore and hurting. Not the most amply endowed of males, he nevertheless managed quite often to release those chilling waves of sheer ecstasy that multiplied into the sense-jangling magnificence of a climax. In turn, she had whispered suggestions to him which had allowed him to improve his technique and to vanquish his problem with premature ejaculation.

122

On days following their successful couplings, Jerry Tibbs had contrived ways to ride as close to her as possible. Hope burned in his eyes for those few occasions when he could get away with breaking Chris Starret's strict instruction not to speak to her except to convey orders. Today had happened to be one of those. As luck would have it, the cavalcade arrived at a water hole some two hours earlier than usual halting time.

"Take ten minutes to refresh," Chris ordered.

Rebecca and her admirer held back as the others dismounted to fill canteens and water their animals. Rebecca could see Jerry fairly burst with the need to say something and she warned him to silence with a finger over her lips.

"Jerry, I've been thinking," she whispered, eyes on Chris rather than the subject of her ploy. "I can't stand to be without you. You being young and able to keep going so many times thrills me. Some night when you have the watch, why don't you release me so I can share it with you? That way you could get an extra turn all to yourself and I could satisfy my urge to have you deep inside me."

Jerry didn't answer, but Rebecca could clearly see her idea working on him by the growing bulge at his crotch. A flicker of pained confusion rippled his smooth, young features and his thin, black eyebrows rose as though startled by something. Chris Starret had had the foresight to bring handcuffs and leg irons for her and, when not riding, or being ridden, she had to endure them. Chris carefully saw to their constant use. By the simple expedient of demanding frequent stops for sanitation needs, she had seen to it that the key was passed from sentinel to sentinel, both day and night. Chris soon tired of being halted, or waking up in the middle of the night and arranged for the present situation.

"Think about it, Jerry. If we're alone, I can take you in my mouth and run my tongue around the tip until your teeth chatter."

Jerry stifled a groan of imagined ecstasy, fighting to keep silent. Given his obvious arousal it wouldn't be long, Rebecca considered smugly.

Big Nose's flesh crawled with goose bumps when he poked his head over the ridge and saw the small band of antelope. His hackles rose when he saw the doe that hopped along on three legs. Suppressing a superstitious dread, he eased the big Remington up and sighted. His single shot dropped her in her tracks. Even as Lone Wolf had predicted, her flanks rippled with fat at the impact of the big .45-90-450 slug. How could the blond medicine man know these things?

When Big Nose found Lone Wolf, he was already on the trail. Not riding, but camped, cooking a meal for Big Nose and himself. Big Nose had been too tired and run down from long days spent in the saddle to wonder why Lone Wolf cooked for two healthy appetites with the sun not yet to the zenith, nor why the mystic's own bedroll was spread for Big Nose to fall into when he'd eaten his fill and told his story. The still unasked question continued to tickle at the back of his consciousness. How had Lone Wolf been so sure? Big Nose's hands flew to the butchering of the barren doe's carcass as he recalled the events of less than an hour ago.

They had been in the trot phase of a walk on foot, trot mounted a mile, then canter a mile and start over march that ate up distance at a rate white men would find hard to believe. The man who had once been Lone Wolf, a Crow brave, turned to Big Nose and said they would catch up with Whirlwind today.

"He will be too starved down to continue the march without red meat. Listen to what I say," Lone Wolf urged. "This morning an antelope doe, who failed to deliver new life this season has broken a leg from carrying too much fat. Climb over this ridge and shoot her. Be sure you shoot the right antelope. She is with a herd and will fall to wolves tonight anyway. Better that we feed her to Whirlwind."

Big Nose was to place the liver in the center of a bundle of meat and wrap it in the hide so it would still be warm when they reached Whirlwind. Working at his task, Big Nose considered the entire chain of events preposterous. Yet he could no more disobey Lone Wolf's instructions than he could doubt the mystic's superior contact with the Spirits.

Hand shaking, Xavier Alvarado poured a jolt of tequila and downed it at a toss. Damn the luck, he should have followed his father's wishes and become a famous matador, like his elder brother. Another hoarse scream ripped the fabric of the dark, velvety evening air that hung heavily around the adobe army post on the outskirts of Celáya, Guanajúato. Xavier cursed again and buckled on his duty belt, with the sabre and .45 Obregon copy of a single action Colt. Damn the luck, he repeated.

He'd recognized the prisoner as the man he'd released, Jose Archuleta, and knew that sooner or later Ordaz's former bandits would have the whole story. There would be retribution. The only question was the form it would take. If Ordaz feared his father's connections in the federal government enough, they might not arrest him. No, in that case, there would be a carefully arranged "accident." That didn't matter, he . . .

The scream came again, ending in a drawn-out series of animal-like grunts that spoke of unendurable pain. Xavier stepped out into the starlight, as the sounds from the tortured man changed into soft, mewling sobs. He made his way to the stables, where he saddled his mare and led her back to a place in the shadows, from which he could see the entrance to his billet.

He hadn't long to wait. A squad of soldiers, under Captain Hector Blancos, all of whom he recognized as close followers of Ordaz, marched up and pounded on his door.

"Xavier! It is Hector Blancos. Come and have a drink with us," the perfidious captain called out in an unctuous voice.

Regretfully, Xavier turned and led his horse off a way, then mounted. Without a backward glance or outward sign of alarm, he rode away to the sound of splintering wood as the heavy panel of his door yielded to the pounding of rifle butts. Xavier held his breath while the sentry passed him through the gate, a moment before the alarm sounded.

At once, the young lieutenant put spurs to his steed. He was an outlaw now, in the bright and proud uniform of a Lancer officer, with no place to go. His father's *granadéria* would be the first place they would look. Tears of rage smarted at his eyes as Xavier thought of the savage indignities he now might bring upon his father and his home. Impulsively Xavier bit at one leather-gloved knuckle in an attempt to have

126

pain drive away the images of suffering his impetuosity in identifying himself to Archuleta as a sympathizer would bring to his family and the peons of Cientó Leguas.

Circumstances, moving too swiftly for him to control or counteract, had forced him into the life of a *bandido,* Xavier at last reasoned. Very well, then, he would live it to the hilt. There was more than one direction in which a bandit could turn his murder and mayhem. With sudden purpose, Xavier turned his mount's head in the direction of the mountains.

A warm, soft breeze blew from the south, still heavy with the moisture of a distant rain shower. Sweet scent rose from wild flowers and sage brush. The time seemed ideal for a romantic tryst. For two more days, Rebecca had busied Jerry Tibbs with graphic, sensuous descriptions of all the erotic pleasures she would provide for him. By now his own urges must be making him frantic, she suspected. Half an hour after the camp settled for slumber, his sudden appearance out of the dark fired her hope.

Signing quiet, he leaned close to her head and whispered. "I'll unfasten one of your hands, if you'll let me hold it. Then we can go talk some more about all those wonderfully wicked things you told me."

"Oh, yes, Jerry, yes," she urged him, kissing his cheek and darting the tip of her tongue into his ear. "Hurry."

He did as instructed and led her to the spot, a hundred yards distant from camp, where he was to keep watch. The leg irons hampered her movement, chafed her ankles, but she said nothing at once. Then

127

in the slight, grassy depression, he began to fondle her.

"Tell me again about how you're gonna take me in your mouth and lick it and kiss it, and make me go wild," Jerry pleaded.

When she began her erotic oratory, his hands delved inside her dress and cupped her breasts. "The nipples, Jerry," she interrupted her salacious soliloquy to instruct. "Squeeze them."

With shaky hands, Jerry complied. Rebecca drew him heartstopping fantasies of lewd and lascivious activity. Despite her conviction that now was the time, she felt her own body responding to the rapacious activities she described. She grew moist, hot and ready. Her breath began to rasp and her mouth went dry. With her free hand she grasped Jerry's rigid, pulsing organ.

Nimbly she unbuttoned his fly and freed the heated, silky shaft and began to rapidly stroke it in the manner he preferred. While she did, she whispered in his ear. "Unlock my leg irons."

The Kid stiffened and eyed her with hurt suspicion. "I can't do that."

"You want to get sucked, don't you? The first time in your life you told me. Well it hurts too much to get on my knees like this. And besides, I want to be able to spread my legs wide and take you deep inside me. You only have to unlock one side."

Hating her hoydenish ploy, Rebecca hoisted her skirt and rubbed his burning penis against her silken belly. She continued to pump him with her warm, soft hand and in a flash, bent low and ran the rough upper surface of her tongue over the blunt, sensitive tip of his throbbing phallus. Jerry groaned and his hips began to undulate.

128

"Do it, Jerry," she urged. "Do it so I can have all of you."

Jerry groaned. "Golly. I, er, ah, oh, golly I think I'm gonna let go now."

"Then I'll stop, while you bend down and loosen my leg. Hurry."

She matched the deed to her words. Jerry hesitated a moment, then hunkered down and fetched the key from his vest pocket. The catch made a loud click as the tumblers released. Eagerly Jerry started upward, senses reeling at her rich, heady womanly scent. The moment he moved, Rebecca swung the loose handcuff with all her strength.

The heavy nickeled brass cuff connected solidly with Jerry's skull. It made surprisingly little noise. Jerry grunted and flopped face first in the grass. Rebecca retrieved the key, shed her irons and removed the Kid's gunbelt. Now actually free, she had to hurriedly examine her plans for this eventuality.

Ample thick brush dotted the area, and before darkness settled down, Rebecca had thought out a means of making it to a heavily forested mountain range prior to sunrise. The alternative plan was for her to try and sort out her horse on this moonless night and run the others off. Indecision plagued her for two precious seconds. At last, she opted to ride. She'd be damned if she would leave her fine palouse stud to a gang of outlaws. Once decided, Rebecca went into instant action.

She bellied out of the grassy wallow and wormed her way around a large boulder. Another thirty yards and she would be at the picket line. She rose, took a firm step, prepatory to starting a low crouching run. Suddenly seized from behind, a hand over her mouth, another on the cylinder of her filched revolver, her attacker bore her to the ground before she could begin to struggle.

Blind rage at so abject a failure engulfed Rebecca and she wriggled in futile effort against the big man on her back. Still reluctant to give up, she bit at his hand as he spoke softly into her ear.

"*Mihunka, nata Nazu Tanka.*"

It was the words in Lakota that began to penetrate, even before Rebecca recognized the voice. Big Nose!

Chapter 13

Only silence came from the camp. The cicadas and crickets had given off their evening serenades. Disturbed by the flap of a night prowler's wings, a bullfrog saluted the darkness with his croak and splashed loudly into the water for protection. Rebecca Caldwell Ridgeway forced herself to relax in the strong arms that held her. An owl hooted from a short distance away.

"You will be quiet?" Big Nose asked.

Rebecca nodded. He released her and they came to their feet. *"Hakamya upo,"* Big Nose whispered, and Rebecca followed him.

Big Nose led her to a rendezvous point. He appeared to be listening to something she could not hear. After a long moment he nodded curtly. A whoop came from the camp. Angry shouts and muzzle flames followed. Then came the pound of hooves and the sound of more shots.

"They are doing well," Big Nose remarked dryly.

"They? Who?" Rebecca pressed, still confused.

"That is Whirlwind. Yes, he's still alive. He and the one who was Lone Wolf are bringing the horses."

A catch in her heart, Rebecca wanted to shout her joy. Whirlwind alive. It seemed impossible. In her excitement over the news of her lover's survival, she failed to note the circumspect reference to Lone Wolf. Thundering closer now, a long string of horses streamed by. At the rear came Whirlwind. There was no sign of Lone Wolf. Whirlwind led Sila. He also had an equally welcome gift. After a quiet greeting, he handed her the brace of Smith and Wesson American revolvers she had so long carried.

"Big Nose brought these from your lodge," Whirlwind told her. "Mount up quickly. We'll drive their horses some distance and then turn away."

Astride their horses, the trio drove the outlaws' horses a good two miles, then headed back to the northwest. When they slowed the pace, Rebecca let the questions spill out.

"Where are the rest of the warriors? With a small number we could finish those border trash in no time."

"It was faster for us to come alone," Whirlwind stated levelly.

He refrained from telling her the real reason. In order to spare her feelings, he and Big Nose had agreed not to mention that although *he* had forgiven her, the men of the band harbored unspoken and unseen resentment against her. The reason being that she had purchased single shot rifles for them, when everyone knew she could have as easily bought them Winchesters.

"What about Lone Wolf? How did he come to be with you?"

"The one who was called Lone Wolf . . ." Big Nose began uncomfortably.

Rebecca interrupted. "You said that before. 'The one who was called' . . . What does that mean?"

Before an explanation could begin, the realization

132

awakened in Rebecca that her old friend had accomplished some sort of spiritual transformation. "It's . . . the Power Road medicine, isn't it?" she asked simply.

Big Nose sighed with relief. "Yes. When I revived Whirlwind, he said to seek out Lone Wolf. It turned out *he* came hunting *me*. He even had food prepared in camp for my arrival. Compared to him, Wolf Brother is a mixer of herbs and a teacher of ritual to small boys."

Whirlwind took up the story, concluding with, ". . . then he had Big Nose wrap the liver in the center of the bundle. When they found me, it was still warm. Lone Wolf sprinkled the meat with a little gall and fed it to me. At once I could feel the strength flow through my body, like life itself returning."

Rebecca noticed their reluctance in speaking of Lone Wolf and considered it with what she already knew. "Is he . . . so different then?"

"I wouldn't say that I am." Appearing suddenly and silently beside the trail, Lone Wolf's words further disconcerted the trio. They exchanged greetings and Lone Wolf spoke again. This time urgency tinged his voice.

"The outlaws are close on our trail, all save the one you struck, Becky. They have recaptured the horses, and are making good time."

"The young one? Did I kill him?" Rebecca inquired with regret.

"No. You simply interrupted communication between his inner spirits. It is the neglect of his companions that will kill him before daylight."

"That's . . . terrible. He really wasn't such a bad sort," Rebecca unconsciously eulogized.

Lone Wolf thought to himself that nothing would be gained by telling her that the separation of his three

133

part spirit entity was permanent. Her blow scrambled what passed for a brain, freeing the middle self from the other two parts. Had the ruthless hardcases not roughed him up and left him beside a cold fire, he would never have been considered "right in the head" again. As it was, he would surely die. In the case of that individual it had been a tragedy. But one not necessary for Rebecca to shoulder.

"Where do we go from here?" Big Nose inquired, his thoughts on their pursuers.

"Roger Styles," Rebecca answered. "He's in Mexico." She quickly explained what she had learned from Chris Starret. "If he wants me there badly enough to send these men after me, perhaps we should go see what's behind it all."

"Just us? The four of us?" Whirlwind inquired, disbelieving.

"Any more would attract attention," Rebecca opined.

"What about those who follow us?" Big Nose asked.

"I have seen that to go north is to ride into danger. Death lies in that direction," Lone Wolf offered. No one needed to ask him how he had "seen" this. "The bandits are now between us and safety with the Red Top Lodge people. It's better if we go south."

"If they continue to follow us, we can at least put a bee in their britches from time to time," Rebecca offered.

"What?" Whirlwind asked, unfamiliar with the white man's idiom.

"Sting them where it hurts most," Rebecca explained. "It's decided, then? I know it's what I want to do."

"It is as my vision showed it," Lone Wolf contributed. "A long journey, with many dangers." He withheld

134

adding, *with death at the end of the trail.*

"We *did not* move too fast!" Roger Styles shouted, red-faced. "These peon uprisings have been common fare for your people since the Spanish Viceroy's time. And I'm not overstepping my perogative to move against Alvarado. Don Estebán may be a *haciendado,* a *hidalgo,* but he is also subject to the laws, as you interpret them," he thundered at Pablo Ordaz.

Met with silence from the latter, Roger broke off to pace the floor of his high-ceilinged study in the *hacienda* of Las Piedras. Not satisfied with a license to steal, Roger Styles had initiated action, through Ordaz and his Federale troops, to seize Alvarado's property. In this instance a large flock of sheep and a herd of cattle, being driven overland to market, to avoid the extortionate freight charges on the railroad. No *ganadéria* could subsist on the sale of two dozen or so fighting bulls each year. Other livestock and crops had to be produced. The restrictions of the "nationalized" spur line had pinched so much as to make it impossible to show a return, let alone a profit. At last, Ordaz felt compelled to speak.

"*Señor* . . . Don Roger, I — we have to answer to the government in Mexico. Don Estebán has powerful friends, some who cannot be bought or intimidated. They, too, have the ear of *el Presidenté.* If enough questions are asked about the railroad . . ." he shrugged expansively.

"You will do as I say," Roger commanded in a low, ominous tone. "You know as well as I that if this does come to the attention of the president, the worst that will happen to us is that Diáz will demand he get a

135

share of the loot. If any of Alvarado's stock gets on the railroad right of way, confiscate what you can. For the rest, have your men scatter them tonight."

Ordaz paled. "Yes, Roger. It will be as you say."

Anger also set the mood at Ciénto Leguas. Don Estebán Alvarado y Polanski wore riding britches, high, cordovan boots and a bolero jacket. A wide, hand-tooled leather belt girded his middle, with a brace of ivory-handled Obregon .45s in smoothly worked holsters. With each forceful step across the stableyard, he slapped a riding quirt into his gloved left palm.

"My son a fugitive, my people lacking all but what we grow here, my bank account dwindling faster than sand castles at high tide. Wouldn't you consider that to be enough for any man to endure, Pépe?"

Pépe Ruiz, the *segundo* of Ciénto Leguas nodded agreement. "Only the tribulations of *nuestro Señor* could be harder to bear, Don Estebán. That paper you were delivered. What does it say?"

"That we cannot drive our livestock across the railroad right of way, Pépe. This is the latest burden given us by that *gringo ladrón.*"

"But the order, it comes from Coronel Ordaz, no?" Pépe asked, confused.

"Pépe, you have seen the voice thrower's *zóquete* at the *circo?* An empty-headed doll whose manipulator makes you believe it is speaking his words. Such is the case with Don Roger Styles and Coronel Ordaz. It is Styles whose greed is behind this. All the same, it is Coronel Ordaz who will carry out the order."

"Then what shall we do?"

"We shall be clever, Pépe. Beginning tonight, and every night after, we will drive small bunches across the right of way. This will be under your direction. Once a respectable herd is built up on the other side, you will take them to market in Morélia. Deposit the money there and go on to Mexico City. I will send with you an authorization to draw on that account and purchase guns. If Styles can't break me, he cannot defeat me. I have been pushed as far as I intend to be."

"What can we do for young Xavier, Don Estebán?" Pépe inquired eagerly.

Don Estebán sighed. "Pray. I'm afraid all we can do now is pray."

For six days Rebecca and her small entourage had moved southwestward. Throughout the time, Chris Starret's outlaws hung close at hand. Now deep into Nebraska, they had the first respite since fleeing the gang in Dakota Territory. Their good fortune could be credited to a small ambush set up for Starret's gang. With one man dead and two severely wounded, Chris held back. It gave Rebecca time to think.

"So far, as we suspected before, we're going the way they want us to. It will also take us to Roger Styles," Rebecca informed her companions. "Chris Starret mentioned several Mexican place names. I don't know if they are cities or states. When we can look at a Mexican map, we can make sure. In the meanwhile, I'd like to get clear of our pursuers."

"How do we do that?" Whirlwind asked.

"We're going to take the train," Rebecca explained. "We'll take passage on the Union Pacific at Fort Kearney, to the junction south of Omaha," she went on.

"There we transfer to the Kansas and Pacific. At Leavenworth, we take the Texas and Great Northern all the way to San Antonio."

Big Nose blinked and tried to settle that in his mind. "We go east, to go south? Why is that?"

"Because it is the only way to quickly get where we want to go. Also it might throw off our pursuers. Sooner or later they have to run out of money, and give up the chase."

"While you still have plenty of gold in that saddle of yours," Whirlwind said proudly.

Rebecca gave him a fleeting frown. "The less said about that, the better. Meanwhile, we might as well plan to travel in luxury. First we get dressed in white man's clothing."

That brought scowls from Whirlwind and Big Nose. Rebecca ignored it. "Then we ride to Fort Kearney to purchase our tickets and tend to the horses."

"We must leave in two days, or they'll catch up with us," Lone Wolf informed her.

"The schedule says tomorrow afternoon," Rebecca replied. "We'll be sure to be ready by then."

"We must go south soon," Lone Wolf continued.

"I want to go back to the Rosebud," Big Nose complained. "All of these whites, their strange ways, I don't like it at all. There is danger here."

"To turn back is certain death," Lone Wolf stated flatly. "To proceed will bring great danger."

"Then what *should* we be doing?" Whirlwind demanded.

"We must go on. This is foreordained. It at least offers us our only hope for survival," Lone Wolf told him.

Lone Wolf had continued to make similar dire prog-

138

nostications since the outset of their journey. Rebecca found herself growing tired of it. Not given to belief in the more esoteric Indian mysticisms, his "other worldly" pronouncements had started to grate.

"You say they are two days behind us," Rebecca referred to Chris Starret's gang. "If we're long gone on the train, I would assume that would take away all of your dark foreboding."

Lone Wolf's face didn't reveal the small pain he felt at her sarcasm. "We must go south. And the danger is there, whether they follow us or not," he answered simply. "Train or no, I don't think modern technology will allow us to outrun our destiny."

Chapter 14

Sweat ran in rivers behind Chris Starret's ears. Heat waves undulated on the Nebraska prairie. They had traveled two hundred miles and to no avail. With three men out of action, no, make it four, what with Kid Tibbs dying on them, he had eight men and no prisoner. Why would they continue to go south?

"I don't understand it," Chris addressed his problem aloud. "I'd almost be willing to think they're going right where we want them." He took a long swig from a half-full canteen of tepid water.

Luke Nelson nodded south. "There's one thing. They might figure to find safety in numbers. The Union Pacific track's only a half day ride south of us. What say they were makin' for that. Catch a train to somewhere with lots of people. Then give us the slip and head back to the reservation?"

"That might be in their minds," Chris said slowly, savoring the idea. "Then again, we all said too much about Roger Styles and Mexico. Could be she's fixin' on some sort of revenge?"

Harry Gonzales-Gonzales chortled pleasantly. "A girl and three men? I would worry more about a shootout with poor Kid Tibbs."

"I favor the railroad," Jim Elkhorn put in.

"They can't have much money, though that fancy stud the girl was riding could buy a lot of miles . . ." Chris formed his thoughts. "We can't dismiss the railroad anyway. Luke, take Anse and three others and split the air between here and the railroad. Get on board the next train, I don't care which way it's going. If they ain't on it, get off at the next station and wait for the one in the opposite direction. Meanwhile, we'll keep on their trail. One or the other of us will catch them and bring an end to it."

"Why are we riding to Don Esteban Alvarado's *ganadería*?" Coronel Pablo Ordaz asked Roger Styles.

A crisp morning made the mountain meadows pleasant. Butterflies swarmed in the cool air, while swallows and flycatchers darted among them to select juicy morsels, then trill brightly over their victories. Here and there the black, brown or speckled white humps of grazing cattle lent a pastoral quality. For all this pacific vista, Roger Styles seethed.

"Somehow he's outsmarted me," he growled. "He has a lot of cattle disappearing and he's not complaining about any thefts. I think I know why."

"How is that?" Ordaz asked.

"He's sneaking out cattle and sheep, slipping them over to the far side of our right of way at night. There's too much line to patrol all of it. Nor can we fence it off effectively. Another thing. Your Don Esteban plans to arm his peons. I learned that from a reliable source inside his faction. That we can't allow."

"We're nearly there now. What if he has already armed them? What if they shoot at us?"

141

"Goddamnit!" Roger shouted. "Your men are supposed to be soldiers. Do what soldiers are supposed to do."

Ordaz shrugged. "Another, ah, 'skirmish with bandits' on my report to Federale Headquarters?"

"Exactly. Only this time, the master bandit of them all had better be one of the casualties. A rebellion is much like a snake. The only way to quell a rebellion is to cut off the head."

Don Esteban Alvarado y Polanski greeted his unwanted visitors with less than cordiality. The insolent manner in which the *gringo* sat his horse irritated enough to demand a satisfaction in blood. Remembering his plans, and his hope for aid, Don Esteban curbed his temper.

"I had heard, Don Esteban, that you were missing some cattle. Sheep, too. I thought it the least I could do," Roger advanced his fiction with oily insincerity, "was to prevail upon the military governor to come over and offer assistance. His troops could perhaps search the hills for you, maybe turn up some bandits."

"You are most kind, Excellency," Don Esteban addressed Roger by his title. "It is a matter of little importance. Only a few head. Perhaps the wolves, or bears have grown fond of a new diet?"

"The way I hear it," Roger pressed, his voice going icy, "is that your difficulty involves nearly eight hundred head of cattle and a thousand sheep. Quite large appetites for wolves or bears, eh?"

"Exaggerations, I assure you." Don Esteban paused abruptly and affected an expression that conveyed chagrin. "Ay, but where are my manners? You must be tired and dusty from your long ride. Do accept the hospitality of my *hacienda*. Come in, refresh yourselves

142

and we will share a glass of good Madiera."

"The perfect host," Roger countered with a subtle sneer.

Face reddening in self-induced anger, Col. Ordaz roared at the elderly *ganádero*. "You would endeavor to insult us, Alvarado? We are not curs to be offered scraps as an afterthought."

"Oh, ah, but no. You misconceive my small social blunder. I err only in my eagerness to assure you that my misfortunes are too insignificant to concern his Excellency and our splendid Military Governor. *Mi casa es su casa.*"

"*Miérde!*" Ordaz bellowed, working himself up nicely now. "Is it that foreign pig of a wife who, before her death, inveigled you to conspire with the common rabble against the authority of your governor?"

Horrified at such an unforgivable insult, Don Esteban could not control the quiver of indignation in his voice. "*Senõr!* You forget yourself. To defame my departed wife is beneath you. She breathed no treason. Nor knew of such."

"I spit on your lies!" Ordaz shouted. "I spit on your wife's grave. Your son an outlaw and rebel, your peons ready to rise up in armed rebellion against my authority, your insincere protests of loyalty and welcome while you machinate behind my back in *La Capital* . . . are we to accept all this as coincidence? I know of your plotting with the merchant class. Watch yourself old man, you are digging your grave with your tongue."

"*Bastante!* If you were a gentleman, instead of a *mestizo* bastard of a bandit, I would demand immediate satisfaction at arms. As it stands, I order you from this place. Get off my land and come back only under pain of death."

"Oho! If it's satisfaction you want . . ." Ordaz hollered gleefully as his Obregon sped from the leather. It made a silver flash as it arced up and outward until the muzzle lined on Estebán Alvarado's face. Yellow-orange flame bloomed outward and a black spot appeared under the tip of the old *ganádero*'s nose.

The bullet angled upward, pulped Don Estebán's brain, and exploded out the back of his skull. Behind him, the faded rose plaster on the wall of the *hacienda* became splattered with droplets of fluid and blood, and gobbets of gray matter. For a long, eerie moment, Don Estebán Alvarado y Polanski stood his ground. Then his proud body slackened, he swayed and fell backward into the dirt of his dooryard.

"Asesino!" a heavy-set woman in a peasant dress and black rebozo shrieked.

Then she turned and ran, sobbing, toward the small church across the plaza. Yelling, frightened peons darted in all directions. Padre Ignacius appeared, wringing his gnarled hands.

"Murderer," he also labeled the burly former bandit, who had as yet to reholster his smoking sixgun.

"Well, you did what we came for," Roger said dryly. "We'd better get on our way. An escort of ten soldiers won't do much against a hundred angry peons."

Ordaz's bloody deed fooled no one. The moment the formation reformed and the hated Federales began a canter along the main road from the *hacienda*, grimly determined men started to gather. Fighting back tears, Manuel Hertado, the *mayóral*, dispatched a rider to the mountains, to locate young Xavier in his hideout and inform him of the tragedy. To the others he gave clear, terse orders.

"Go for your weapons. Those of you who have them,

get your rifles and all the ammunition you can gather. Arturo, ride to the villages and tell them. The merchants will help arm all of you. We will all gather here. Then we will decide where and when we shall turn their tan uniforms red with their own blood."

Fort Kearney, Nebraska looked like any other white community built up around a military post. More attention had been paid to providing creature comforts to the off-duty soldiers, than in laying out a neat, orderly city. In other words, Rebecca Caldwell Ridgeway summed it up, the proximity to the main gate and number of saloons and whorehouses had taken priority over logic. The streets had not even been named. Yet Fort Kearney did have a Union Pacific railroad depot.

"We have plenty of time," Rebecca informed her companions when they halted on the outskirts of town. "We'll get our tickets and arrange for the horses to be put on board. But first we have to get white people's clothing."

Whirlwind and Big Nose gave her looks of rebellion. She hastened to explain. "They won't let us on the train otherwise."

Rebecca dismounted and slit open the bottom of one decorative, rolled leather piping on a fender of her saddle. From it she removed a fine trickle of gold dust that added up to a nice stake. She secured this in a small leather poke and rummaged in her saddle bags. While the men conversed in low tones, she shook out a print dress and changed into it, added button shoes and a bonnet, then swung atop Sila.

"I have a fair idea of your sizes," she informed her friends. "Boots for all of you, hats, shirts, trousers and

145

vests," she ticked off like a haberdashery clerk.

"Please," Lone Wolf interrupted, "no ties."

Rebecca laughed lightly. "No neckties, agreed. I should be back in half an hour. Once you've changed, we'll go get the tickets, have something to eat and be ready to take the train."

Much to Rebecca's relief, her transactions went smoothly. Once the men had dressed in civilized clothing, it appeared that a white couple, Lone Wolf and Rebecca, were traveling with a pair of Delaware "breeds." At the depot, they secured passage for themselves and their horses, through to Leavenworth, Kansas. There they would have to buy tickets on the Texas and Great Northern. Lone Wolf pointed out a convenient cafe, where they dined without incident. At one-fifteen that afternoon, they returned to the depot.

With her party standing by to load their livestock, Rebecca watched detachedly as the eastbound Union Pacific rolled slowly onto the siding and stopped with the cattle cars in the stockyards, the passenger cars at the station. Several passengers clambered off, some to loud greetings by family or friends. Others made ready to board. Among those who remained aboard were five suddenly excited outlaws.

"That's her, only in real clothes," Jim Elkhorn declared. "Look up there where they're loadin' horses."

"Are you sure?" Luke Nelson asked, expectation growing.

"Of course I am," Jim snapped.

"Then we've got to get out of here. Unload the horses from the other stock car so we can make a getaway with the girl," Luke advised. "Anse, you see to that, the rest of us will go after that white squaw."

Quickly they dispersed to their duties. Less than a

minute later, Anse Angleton faced a stubbornly determined conductor. Like a bantam rooster, the trainman stood up to the hard-faced outlaw.

"Nope. Can't do that. Ain't no train order to off-load livestock here. We picked up a slip on loadin' four horses, I can show you that. But we can't lose any more time takin' yours off. Enough of a damn problem puttin' them on at that jerkwater station this mornin'."

"Mister, I mean business," Anse growled.

Hands on hips, the conductor faced him down. "They ain't comin' off and that's final."

We'll just see, Anse thought to himself as he turned away and stalked off up the track, leaving the conductor behind. "Jim, Harry, gimme a hand," he called out to the closest of the gang.

At Anse's call, Rebecca recognized the loathsome hardcase and halted the others. Their mounts had already been loaded and they had started toward the passenger cars. "I don't know how they did it, but that's one of them. Anse Angleton. We're going to have to shake them first."

"What about our horses?" Whirlwind asked.

"They'll be held for us in Omaha. We have to lead Angleton and the rest off, then get the next train. The stockyards. We'll go that way. Maybe we can ambush them there," Rebecca suggested.

Anse broke the railroad seal on the stockcar door and rolled it back. He and the other two outlaws entered. Quickly they hurled saddles out onto the freight platform, then slipped bridles on all five horses. They swung atop three, and led the remaining pair as they rode out the door onto the platform.

"They headed for the stockyards," Luke Nelson called from a short distance away.

Amid great confusion of offended passengers, an outraged crew, and nervous animals, the gang saddled up and prepared to charge the cattle pens. Directly ahead of them, the engineer had seen what was happening. Anger at this high-handed activity, and furious over the delay it would cause, he had been waiting for the right moment to express his opinion of the proceedings. As the hardcases swung legs over their mounts, the engineer's hand closed over a brass handle. With a stout yank, he vented a hissing roar of steam across the platform in front of them.

Five horses went berserk. One sunfished, while two crow-hopped in widening circles. Another ran head-first into a 4 x 4 support post and the roof over the platform sagged dangerously. Half on their terrified and pitching mounts, the outlaws quickly became more than half off. Shrill whinnies drowned out the final eruption of steam. With firm concentration, Luke Nelson, then Jim Elkhorn, followed by the rest, managed to regain their seats and recover a modicum of control. With bucks and snorts, the outlaw charge went on.

"They're coming," Lone Wolf announced.

"We don't have our horses," Big Nose lamented.

"Which gives us the advantage," Rebecca informed him. "We can move faster on foot than they can by horse. We can cross corrals, while they have to ride around. We'll find a good place, then ambush them one by one."

"Where are they?" Anse Angleton yelled.

"Over there somewhere," Jim Elkhorn replied, pointing to the corrals.

148

"There, I saw a flash of that red skirt," Connor Quinn shouted, pointing.

A great deal more confusion developed while the outlaws tried to locate a route through the maze of corrals. Luke caught sight of a coppery face and fired. Powder smoke mingled with the thick dust of straw, dirt and dried cattle manure as the others reflexively opened up. Cattle rolled eyes until only the whites showed and bawled in terror, while horses screamed and stampeded around the pens. For a moment, no one saw anything of the opposing side.

"Over there," Anse Angleton shouted, rising in his saddle. Strangely enough, no bullet came to cut him down.

"Jim, you and Connor go that way," Luke ordered. "We'll cut 'em off."

Their ambush site seemed well-chosen. Whirlwind had led them there, on the north side of the stockyard. They crouched low keeping well out of sight. Whirlwind moved forward to open a gate. In an instant, outlaws appeared from seemingly every direction. Rebecca and her companions had so far held their fire, for worry over striking innocents behind the gunmen. Now they had a clear field of fire.

Anse Angleton appeared over the sights of the Smith American in Rebecca's hands. A particular delight, born of memories of his brutal lust, brightened her face as she squeezed the trigger. As though jerked by a string, Anse's hat flew into the air, followed by a spray of hair, hide, bone and blood.

Reflexively Anse jerked backward, wavered and fell from his horse. Despite the loss of one man, incoming

149

fire increased in volume. Rebecca ducked low and started to move to a safer place. A shout startled her and caused her to spin around.

"Sinaskawin, behind you!" Whirlwind bellowed.

Before Rebecca completed her turn, a sixgun blasted from close at hand. Gobbets of something wet splattered her face. Suddenly she realized they were pieces of Whirlwind's forehead and brains. Gagging, she stumbled to one side, which saved her from the second shot fired by Jim Elkhorn.

"This way," Lone Wolf called, preventing Rebecca the opportunity to avenge her lover's death.

Bent low, screened by terrified cattle and hysterical horses, Rebecca, Lone Wolf and Big Nose sprinted along a walkway in the direction of the train. The whistle called to them, the signal for all aboard. With a painful wrench to her heart, Rebecca remembered Whirlwind's body.

"We've got to go get him," she pleaded.

"We can't . . ." Lone Wolf started, then changed his mind. "You stand them off, we'll take care of it." He and Big Nose started out.

Rebecca continued to fire at the dodging, weaving figures of the pursuing outlaws, One took a wound. Then, from behind her, she heard the reports of several weapons. A quick look reassured her. The railroad people had joined the fight, and on her side. With lifted spirits, she increased her fire.

Overwhelming odds left little choice for Luke Nelson and his remaining pals. He signaled and they spun away from the fusillade. Riding swiftly as the packed corrals would permit, they made hasty retreat. They already dwindled in size on the prairie when Lone Wolf and Big Nose returned with Whirlwind's body.

150

"We'll have to stay here and answer questions," Rebecca opined. "Which should give us time to . . . to bury him."

Anger had shoved grief aside. Roger Styles had caused this, surely as though he had pulled the trigger himself. She would hunt him down, drag him from his lair in Mexico and kill him with her bare hands if necessary. Mentally constructing a hot wall of hate, she isolated the cold pit of sorrow. There would be time for mourning later. Now she had a job to do.

Chapter 15

Never had the clouds streaming through the passes of the Sierra Madre seemed so black. The very air felt liquid and weighty. Lt. Xavier Ernesto Alvarado y Polanski gazed at the towering columns, their fat bellies laden with rain. He sighed heavily and tried to find some reason in the recent, fast-moving events. His father murdered, shot down by a bandit pig not worthy to clean the elder Alvarado's boots. When tyrants like Diaz reigned, criminals flourished, and good men suffered. Scalding anger rose to push aside the sorrow.

All the philosophizing in the world would not remove the fact that Pablo Ordaz had to die. Although technically his superior, Xavier considered it a blood debt to see that the bandit-turned-Federale paid for his unspeakable crime. Xavier turned abruptly from the ledge where he stood, putting behind him the awesome power of nature. With swift, sure strides he returned to where the messenger waited.

Young Jaime Quintal had brought word of the terrible event. Xavier approached him now, his face clouded with a scowl. "Return to Ciento Leguas," Xavier instructed. "Tell Manuel Hertado to bring what arms he has been able to obtain. Filipe," he went on, referring to the *alcalde* of the ranch's principal village, Filipe Chacón, "is to remain behind, in charge. He is to turn the flocks, herds, and fields over to the boys, eight to fourteen years of age. All others, Manuel is to organize and bring here, with you as guide. Is everything understood?"

"*Clarito, Don* Xavier," young Jaime responded, his round straw hat clasped in both hands, pressed to his chest.

"Then get something to eat, take some food for your journey, and get on your way," Xavier snapped off, the habit of command returning through the miasma of his grief.

Fully half of Xavier's men had deserted, to join him in the mountains of Guanájuato, along with a small band of twenty *macheteros* whom he had recruited. More arrived all the time, though not enough to be an effective force against the well-equipped troops of Pablo Ordaz. So far Xavier had received provisions from his father's *ganadéria*. The news of his father's death changed his priorities. His immediate problem now became the means of feeding the growing number of dissidents. To that end, he assembled his subordinate leaders.

"Word of a tragedy travels quickly. You no doubt know of my father's murder by Pablo Ordaz. That is behind us now," Xavier dismissed. "We must have supplies; food, medicine, arms and ammunition. To get them, we will conduct raids on the friends of *Coronel* Ordaz, and his overlord, Roger Styles."

"*Acerca de tiémpo,*" Tomás Guevera exclaimed.

Cousin of the betrayed Ernesto Guevera, El Tiburón, Tomás came to Xavier's call fired with zeal. Xavier resented the youth's interruption, expecting it to result in another philosophical harangue that fired

153

the men's spirits, but resulted in little accomplishment. In his childhood, not but a few years behind, Tomás had been carefully taught by his revolutionary cousin. This Xavier learned shortly after Tomás joined his outlaw band. Ernesto had provided the materials and instructed Tomás in reading and writing, also in the principles of Marx.

Spoon-fed on the untried Marxian theory, the impressionable boy had become an adult true believer. What irritated Xavier most of all was that Tomás considered his departed elder cousin some sort of revolutionary saint. Shortly after the short, slender, disturbingly intense young man arrived, he began preaching his form of the discredited European doctrine to the rebels. Xavier spoke to him about it and the deep-seated resentment and fanatical zeal that fired Tomás built up into a shouting fit of vituperation and an exhortation to abandon all present forms and embrace the "wisdom of the ages, the tide of the future."

Xavier found himself in a quandary regarding Tomás. Tomás could read and write, he organized his thoughts and actions well. Xavier needed officers, which made it more difficult. And now he must deal with another outburst.

" 'About time' for what?" he demanded.

"Why, the redistribution of wealth, Comrade Leader," Tomás responded smugly. "Take from the degenerate capitalists and give to the workers."

"The proper term of address is *Capitán, Teniente* Guevera. And, I fail to see how stealing cattle, goats and sheep, to feed us is providing anything to the workers. We need weapons, ammunition and food, as I stated originally. We're going to get them by taking what we want from those who support our enemy."

"We must do more than that. We have to tear down

154

the bastions of capitalism to make way for the great society of the proletariat."

Xavier doubted if Tomás even knew the definition of *proletariat*. He fastened a grip on his pique. "Our purpose is to bring down a tyrant who has oppressed us all, not to replace him with a new tyranny of some foreign ideology."

"You cannot deny the truth of what Marx says . . ."

"I can, and I do. In the end, Tomás, it is all theory, and Marx is but one of many we studied at the university," Xavier explained in an attempt to mollify his junior officer. "I can also remind you this is a meeting for officers. Your presence here was commanded, it can be rescinded. Spare us your oratory, or return to your duties and make ready for a raid on the Sandina *estancia* tonight," Xavier snapped, letting slip a corner of his temper.

What a shame, he reflected, how a little knowledge can become a dangerous thing. Tomás was a good man, an idealist, and fiercely loyal. Too bad his passions had been misdirected. Utopian theories had come and gone since the time of the ancient Greeks, Xavier ruminated. None were inherently evil. Yet, without the balance wheel of a solid grounding in the classics, in Latin, Greek, in Aristotle's logic, and the history of the Western World, how terribly flawed any attempt at application could become. God help us if the day ever comes when the classics are not read in the schools, or deliberately misrepresented. How deadly such miseducation would become. Then gossamer theory, like that of this *judeo* Marx, might take the place of logic and reason and the world would be plunged into darkness. With an effort, Xavier shook himself free of such gloomy thoughts.

"Gentlemen, we will begin our raids tonight."

Devastated by the death of Whirlwind, Rebecca grew more withdrawn, so that by the time they reached Omaha, she barely communicated. They had retrieved the Oglala warrior's body from the stockyard. After hours of questioning, in which the train left without them, they arranged for a Sioux burial. It took place the next morning and, at last, the saddened trio boarded the eastbound train. They had neither seen nor heard anything about the remaining outlaws seeking them. In Omaha, Rebecca deferred to Lone Wolf's decisions without comment. Big Nose had become so in awe of the mystic that to doubt the seeming urgency of continuing southward would not have occurred to him. After a day and a half layover in Omaha, they boarded the Kansas and Pacific steamer to Leavenworth.

Depression began to give way to a smoldering anger for Rebecca. Her mind had begun to whirl with questions, problems and the images of the past. How could fate be so cruel? To be deprived of her two great lovers within a short span of two years seemed more than even the stern, forbidding, and vindictive God of the Jews and Christians would demand. She fought the feeling of being cut adrift from reality. Why must they go south? *Roger Styles,* a blinding rage answered her. Ultimately, he had the responsibility for Whirlwind's death. What of Joey? Alone now and living as a Sioux boy among the Oglala, in another man's lodge, a boy willing to grow up as a Sioux warrior, rather than a white man's child. He needed a better life than that, Rebecca conceded. What better life?

Her unanswered questions served only to build her fury. She began to look forward to confronting Roger

Styles. The miles and days rolled on. Somewhere in Texas, Rebecca began to note that her health and mental processes were being gradually restored. Out of the haze of her week-long misery, she responded to a question.

"Roger has no idea we're coming after him. Even if his bully dogs succeed in relaying word of my escape, neither they nor he would expect me to head toward Mexico."

"Aren't we taking a risk, going down through the center of Mexico to where Roger is supposed to be?" Lone Wolf inquired.

"You're the seer. What do you envision for us?" Rebecca answered tartly. Instantly she regretted her lack of tact. "That was rude of me, Lone Wolf. I'm sorry. Actually, even if he suspected I, we, were after him, he'd hardly expect us to come at him head on. Much too direct, Roger would figure. Since he performs his evil deeds against a background of conspiracy and deceit, he would naturally expect others to function the same way."

Warmed by her ring of confidence and glib manner, Lone Wolf eased his intense questioning. The train made better time. The number of isolated ranches and depots grew fewer and farther between as the Texas and Great Northern rocked down the track toward San Antonio. The "milk run" as she had heard people call it, chugged along at a breath-taking fifty miles an hour. They reached San Antonio an hour before sundown.

With horses, tack and luggage recovered, they set out to find lodging. Half a block down the street, a policeman accosted them. "What are chu doeeng weeth a savage in thees town?" he asked in a thick Mexican accent.

His night stick tapped Big Nose on the chest. For a

157

moment, Rebecca thought Big Nose might snatch it away from him and break it over his head. She spoke quickly to defuse the situation.

"He's not a savage, he's a half-breed, and a civilized one at that. He works for us."

Still dubious, the policeman examined all three. "Chu wear buckskin trousers, like the old timers," the cop said to Lone Wolf. "Not many in San Antonio do that. What chu do for a leeving?"

"We guide pilgrims out into Kansas and Colorado," Lone Wolf answered simply.

"We've come south on a sort of holiday," Rebecca added.

"An' thees one work for you? Of course he can speek English?"

"Of course he can," Rebecca began. Then Big Nose cut her off with some of his few choice words in that language.

"Fugg you so'jer."

To Rebecca's surprise, the policeman laughed. "I have wanted . . . to say . . . that so many . . . times," he choked out through the chuckles. Then he sobered. "Your breed friend cannot be out on the street at night. Chu must find him a place to stay."

"What about where we take rooms?" Rebecca inquired.

"Oh, definitely not inside. It is forbidden. Unless they have a stable he can stay there," the cop provided.

"Thank you very much," Lone Wolf injected. "We'll take care of it right away."

"Why did you do that?" Rebecca demanded. "I think he had a lot of nerve, saying Big Nose couldn't stay where he wanted to, or go out at night. I was going to tell him what I thought."

"And get us all thrown in jail?" Lone Wolf chuckled.

158

Actually he saw her defensive anger as a good sign.

"What *awful* people," Rebecca snapped.

Rebecca's Spanish, although rusty since her sojourn in California, secured them accommodations at the *Pósada Alamo*, across the moon-speckled surface of the San Antonio River from the ruins of the historic mission compound. Border Spanish, or Tex-Mex, as some were beginning to call it, proved to be the *lingua franca* of the area. Early the next morning, when Rebecca and Lone Wolf seated themselves at a table for breakfast, their blonde, blue-eyed waitress addressed them first in Spanish.

"*Buenas diás. Su queres deseyuno, o café solo?*"

"Er — ah, *deseyuno, por favor*," Rebecca replied hesitantly. "Er — *jamon con*, ah, *huevos, pan-panécillo . . .*"

"Oh, excuse me. What would you like for breakfast?" the waitress responded when she heard Rebecca's stumbled response.

Rebecca gave her a beaming smile. "Thank you. Ham and eggs, biscuits, gravy, and grits. With a side of apple pie."

"What do you eat when you're really hungry?" Lone Wolf asked, recalling her remark when he called for her at her room. Actually he felt heartened by her sudden spurt of appetite. "I'll take the steak, blue-rare, biscuits, and any fresh fruit you have."

"Coffee for both of you?" the yellow-locked girl inquired routinely.

"I will," Rebecca replied.

"Water, please," Lone Wolf ordered.

"*Water?* You mean, to drink?" the startled waitress blurted.

"Yes, of course, I've already taken a bath," Lone Wolf answered, blank faced.

Shaking her head at the weird quirks of some

people, their waitress went off to place the order.

"We have to plan on what to do from here," Rebecca began after coffee arrived. Her rekindled interest filled her with vitality.

"First we have to get into Mexico," Lone Wolf offered.

"Given that, then what?" Rebecca waited in silence, while Lone Wolf avoided an answer, hoping to draw her out. At last she made the final leap into her old self.

"I think we should take the fastest way south. That means back on the train."

"How far can we go?" Lone Wolf inquired.

"I'm . . . not sure. There is a train from Nuevo Laredo to Monterrey, I learned last night. Surely the track runs further than that. We'll take it as far as we can."

Big Nose, like the lower class Mexicans and the Negroes, could not be served in a place so fine as where Rebecca and Lone Wolf dined. Nor would he wish to be, he considered sensibly. From a small stand made of cane and poles, under a palmetto leaf *palapa,* he purchased a large hunk of juicy, smoking-hot meat. Held in a wrap of three large corn tortillas, he ate both meal and plate with smiling gusto.

"Carne de perró," the grinning entrepreneur informed him.

Big Nose looked back blankly. The street-corner chef grinned all the more and pointed to a stray dog passing by. *"Carne de perró."*

A huge smile blossomed on Big Nose's face, making it highly mobile. He nodded his understanding vigorously. *"Hau-hau, sunka wana waste. Pila maye,* thank you," he repeated in Lakota, wishing to express his gratitude for the special effort this stranger had made on his part.

Astonished at this favorable reaction by so obvious a stranger, the vendor felt a moment's flash of disappointment. He'd seen many a foreigner, mostly gringos, turn pale, then green, and then lose all they had consumed when advised that the puppies of the town had provided their repast. This fellow, on the other hand, seemed all right.

"Querés mas?"

It didn't take any talent for linguistics for Big Nose to figure out that one. *Of course* he wanted more. Nodding and smiling, he put out his hands, one of which still held a warm, grease-slicked tortilla. The street cook fished into his pot, swilling the brownish liquid, and came up with another hunk, fully as big as the last. He added tortillas, a dash of salt and a sprinkle of ground chili.

Big Nose slurped and smacked his appreciation. When he finished, he licked his fingers and dug out a silver dollar. The vendor tried to explain that he offered too much. Big Nose didn't understand. *Sinaskawin* had explained that in the white man's world, everything must be paid for with the white man's money discs.

"Diez centavos," the vendor insisted. "Only tan cen's," he repeated in English. He showed Big Nose a dime.

"Pila maye," Big Nose stated and replaced the cartwheel, he groped for a ten cent piece and proudly handed it to the man.

"You come back again," the vendor urged.

Big Nose nodded uncomprehendingly and walked off.

Chapter 16

Emerald green and looking pugnacious, a lizard did pushups on a warm rock, black BB eyes fixed on the curious cavalcade stopped by the side of the road. Its tongue flickered a few times, savoring the vibrations in the air. A short distance away, two gophers made steady advances at enlarging their tunnel system. As if by magic, finely ground dirt appeared at the one visible entrance to their burrow. Even these primitive creatures could sense the tension building around the large beings near by.

"One wagon, three horses, a mestizo driver an' two Chewnited States citizens. How long do you stay in Mexico?" the tan-uniformed official demanded.

"We're not certain," Rebecca responded. "We want to take the train from Nuevo Laredo to Monterrey, then on to Mexico City."

Irritated at being addressed by a woman, the inspector feigned not understanding. "Tran? What is tran?"

"The, ah, *ferrócarril*," Rebecca supplied.

"Oh, *sí*. That railroad does not run past Monterrey," their interrogator advised.

"We know. We have to change in Monterrey."

"There are many bandits in those mountains, *Señora*,"

162

came the hint.

"We should be safe enough on the train," Rebecca surmised.

"Quien sabe?" the inspector responded with a shrug. "This, ah, *mestizo* of yours? He is part Apache, no?"

"No, sir. He's Delaware, one of the civilized tribes," Lone Wolf put in, sensing the friction between the *macho*-driven inspector and the alluringly feminine Rebecca.

"I am Christian Injun," Big Nose slurred in English.

The inspector nodded, as if that explained everything satisfactorily. He scribbled on the notepad he held and waved them on. "All is in order. You may enter Mexico. But be careful of bandits."

With a beaming smile and casual wave, Rebecca led off on Sila. Before they went to the railroad depot, the trio made a detour by two important establishments. First they purchased bacon, beans, rice and a tub of lard, enough for a three week stay. At a shop down the street they stocked up on ammunition and Lone Wolf added a case of dynamite to their stores. Word of their presence, and their actions, passed rapidly through the small town.

Three Mexican officials waited for them at the gate in the tall rock and wrought iron fence outside the depot. "One moment, please," the leader demanded, his hand out as though directing traffic.

"Yes? What is it?" Lone Wolf answered.

"We must search your belongings."

"What are you saying?" Rebecca asked heatedly. "Do you have a warrant?"

The youngest of the uniformed trio snickered. "What ees a war'an'?"

"Dismount and allow us to search your supplies," the

163

leader repeated.

Rebecca and Lone Wolf exchanged glances, shrugged and dismounted. Quickly and efficiently, the policemen prowled through their possessions. They made much over the stored rifles, cases of ammunition and the dynamite. Then the heavy-set one turned his attention to Big Nose. He spoke in an agitated whisper to the leader, who smiled nastily and nodded.

"It seems you have committed several serious crimes," he addressed to Lone Wolf. "First is the smuggling of arms, a most heinous offense. Then there is the matter of this Apache. There is a bounty on their scalps in this country, didn't you know?"

"He is not an Apache," Rebecca stated with rising heat.

"Me Delaware," Big Nose said flatly.

"With that nose, you are Apache to me, my frien'," the fat one leered.

The leader shrugged. "All Indians look alike. Do you have any proof of his origins? Some, ah, document?"

By then, Rebecca had clearly read their intentions. Oh, she and her companions would be arrested right enough, if they didn't satisfy these men. Yet they were after something else, not just an impressive arrest record for the day. She delved into her waist pouch as she spoke.

"We haven't a birth certificate, if that's what you mean. To check out the truth of our story will take some time and expense, isn't that so? Well, we have a train to catch. Perhaps if we were to underwrite the expense of an investigation, you could conduct it after we're aboard the train?"

She withdrew a wad of currency and peeled off a trio of hundred peso notes. Blank as polished obsidian, three pairs of eyes stared fixedly at the money. Rebecca added another, then another. When six hundred pesos rested on the palm of one hand, the leader produced a smile and nodded.

"Such matters are expensive, *que no?* Your understanding is appreciated. It is likely we will be able to clear this up in a day or two." He reached out swiftly and made the bills disappear. "Meanwhile there is no reason to cause undue delays for our *Norteño* friends. Have a good trip to Monterrey. *Adios.*"

"It's shocking to see you bribe agents of a foreign government like that," Lone Wolf remarked after the shake-down officials departed. "It's also a risky proposition."

"Not at all," Rebecca defended herself. "The whole country runs on *mordida,* the bite. I learned that from Alonzo Horton, in San Diego."

"But you took a chance that they would be honest men, or offended by the amount you offered," Lone Wolf challenged.

"Hardly. It's a matter of balancing their zeal against their greed. If they did arrest us and confiscate our possessions, they would have had to share the proceeds with their superiors. By taking the bribe, they got to keep it all."

"Bribery is immoral. It blocks communication with the High Self," her longtime friend said without a hint of smugness.

"It's the way of life in Mexico," Rebecca held her line.

A hint of a smile lifted the corners of Lone Wolf's mouth. "Then let's hope you continue to strike the right balance."

He turned his head abruptly to hide the outward signs of his secret pleasure. Rebecca had begun to show enough spunk so that he felt sure she had recovered from the worst of her grief. When they did encounter Roger Styles, she would be ready.

"I understand that this will be our last meeting, Coronel Von Ritter," Pépe Ruíz, *ségundo* for Ciento Leguas stated flatly as he took a chair at a heavy, ornately carved table at the rear of the patio of the Casa Fernandes, an exclusive restaurant in Mexico City.

"That is correct," Joachim Von Ritter responded. He signaled for the waiter to bring them a pre-selected bottle of wine.

An advisor to the Mexican army, *Herr Oberst* von Ritter enjoyed a privileged position. The tall, thin, Teutonic aristocrat cut a striking figure among the short-statured citizens of the capital city, indeed of all Mexico. He wore his splendid Prussian uniform with a flare that indicated anything else would be drab and unattractive on his broad-shouldered frame. He adjusted his monocle and peered at the two sheets of paper before him.

"Fifty thousand pesos . . ." he began, then paused as the waiter approached with their refreshment.

When the white-jacketed attendant departed, he repeated himself. "Fifty thousand pesos converts to fifteen thousand, eight hundred *Deutschmarks*. A sufficient sum to purchase several cases of our 1871/84 Mauser rifles. They are remarkable firearms. Here, let me show you." von Ritter signaled again and a subordinate across the room walked to their table, bearing one of the rifles.

"This weapon fires the eleven millimeter cartridge.

The bullet size and weight is ideal for a military arm. The powder charge adequate to insure accuracy at ranges up to four hundred meters. The rifle has a nine-shot, tubular magazine with a cutoff mechanism. This allows it to be fired single shot, without depleting the magazine, which is thus held in reserve to beat off a major charge, or meet other emergencies. Also, that guarantees that a soldier will not accidently shoot up all of his ammunition without ending an engagement with at least a nine shot reserve."

"Magnificent!" Pépe enthused. He well knew the propensity of peons to expend all their cartridges, throw down their weapon and desert the field in the face of superior, disciplined fire.

Joachim von Ritter continued extolling the virtues of the 11mm Mauser. "The sights are of the pyramid and V-notch variety, with a ladder rear that is adjustable for both windage and elevation. No more guessing, or as the Americans put it, 'Kentucky windage.' Notice the quality of the machining. The wood-to-metal fit is outstanding and the rifle has a comfortable feel to it. Here, try it." Von Ritter handed the long, sturdy rifle to Pépe.

Ruíz shouldered the piece, pressed his cheek to the stock. Although heavy, it had a fine balance and did not stretch his trigger finger to the utmost to make contact. "Excellent. When can I take delivery?"

Colonel von Ritter pulled a wry face. "This is not exactly a, ah, sanctioned sale. Such things take time. Your line of credit drawn on this account," again von Ritter nodded toward the papers, "has been acknowledged by the bank, which will shorten that some. I would say several days, perhaps five or six."

More likely weeks, the *segundo* considered, given the

mañana attitude of Mexico. "Who will be handling them?"

"Only my people. You understand that though your country's army will hardly be harmed or inconvenienced by the disappearance of so few rifles, since the fools issue them to garrison troops around the capital and few, if any, reach units in the field, and that the fewer who know of this the better. You will be notified at your hotel when the shipment arrives from Veracruz. Thank you very much. It's a pleasure dealing with you. *Auf Wiedershen.*"

South of Monterrey now, headed for San Luis Potósi, the powerful American Locomotive Works 2-6-0 engine pulled the twelve car string at a remarkable speed. Great mountains, built of immense boulders and rich soil, all in reds and browns, slid past the windows of the first class car. Although grimy with years of neglect, the glass panels provided a spectacular display.

Rebecca Caldwell Ridgeway lost herself in the vista of a land she had never before seen. The trees were stunted, gnarled and twisted by nearly ceaseless wind. Here and there some family had gouged out a living spot, with partially leveled fields to produce scraggly crops of corn, beans, onions, and the ubiquitous chili peppers. Tomato vines climbed lattice arms on the walls of houses.

Frequently the train had to slow or halt to allow flocks of goats and sheep to cross the grade, driven by hordes of nearly naked little boys. The youngsters grinned and mugged for the passengers and waved in a friendly way. In other places settlements had been hacked out of the hard, hostile mountain slopes. Here a church spire raised to the heavens, a few two story buildings could be seen, and the children appeared in greater profusion. Rarely did the train stop to take on passengers. So great was the poverty of the people that few had the pesos to spare for a ticket. As the altitude increased, the desert vegetation gave way to conifers and aspen, large green meadows, like shallow jade bowls, dotted the slopes.

"We'll be stopping at Vanégas to take on water and coal," Lone Wolf informed his companions. "Half an hour there to get something to eat."

"Something other than cold tamales and tacos, you mean," Rebecca spoke up. "The food here is good, and filling. But I'm certain it's intended to be eaten warm. I'll be glad for a chance to sit down, eat off a plate and use regular utensils."

"Going 'civilized' on us, Becky?" Lone Wolf teased.

Hoist by her own petard, Rebecca managed to stammer a reply. "Oh, you know what I mean."

A tall, handsome Anglo, whom they had seen often before, made his way down the aisle, toward the trio. He paused and removed his hat. "Hello, I'm Mark McDade."

His smile was wide, white and winning, his wavy blond hair cut to perfection and combed neatly into place. He wore an expensive suit of pearl gray, with thin blue pinstripes, a spotless white shirt and rakish foulard tie.

"How do you do?" Rebecca responded. "I am Rebecca Caldwell Ri—ah, and this is Brett Baylor. Also our friend Big Nose."

"Ummmm. What an odd name. Big Nose, I mean, not Rebecca. I don't mean to pry, but are you traveling far?"

"Only to San Luis Potósi," Lone Wolf informed him.

"Aaah. There's a lot of unrest around that area right now. Not a good place to be, alone that is. I'm at loose ends because of it. I'm a mining engineer and the quarrels between some of the *haciendados* and the military government drove me from my job."

"We're only visitors," Rebecca dismissed. "We're looking for an old friend."

"Forgive me, I'm not trying to sign onto your expedition, no matter how it sounds. I'm enjoying a bit of holiday. If you told me the name of your friend, I might be able to help locate him. We may be acquaintances."

"Roger Styles," Rebecca stated, each syllable grating.

Young McDade's cordial manner changed abruptly. His eyelids dropped over deep blue eyes and he spoke with a distinct coolness in his tone. "I, ah, see. Roger Styles is a special envoy for President Diaz. I'm afraid I don't travel in those circles. Now, if you'll excuse my intrusion, I must be going."

"Don't, please," Rebecca started, but it was too late. Mark McDade's broad back moved away down the aisle toward the door to the observation platform. Impulsively, Rebecca rose and followed him.

Although noisy, the observation platform at the rear of the first class car had an exhilarating quality about it. Buffered from the slipstream of the train, one could stand against the rear wall of the car, or out at the rail and watch the scenery go by in a panoramic view. Rebecca waited several minutes, marshaling her thoughts, before she stepped forward and lightly touched Mark McDade's coat sleeve.

"Excuse me, Mister McDade. I feel you have a right

to an explanation."

"None needed, nor wanted. Friends of Roger Styles are hardly friends of mine."

"Nor ours, actually. I'm afraid we weren't entirely truthful with you. Oh, we're looking for Roger all right. Only, if you knew me, you'd be aware I'm far from a friend of his."

"Oh? Why should I believe that?" Mark asked defensively.

"Because, on five separate occasions, I've tried to kill him," Rebecca stated flatly.

McDade's eyebrows raised. "You? A, ah, beautiful young lady like you tried to kill Roger Styles?"

"*Yes.*" Such vehemence transmitted veracity far better than words. "It's a long story, and I'd be glad to tell you all of it, if the train ride is long enough. Suffice that I have spent the better part of my adult life pursuing Roger Styles and the men in an outlaw gang he commanded up in the United States."

Still dubious, Mark commented, "That's some undertaking."

"All of them, except Roger, are in prison, or dead. Mostly dead."

"And you . . . ?"

Unsure of herself for the first time since the conversation began, Rebecca looked away from Mark. "I did. I even pulled the trigger bar on the trap of the gallows that hanged one of them in Fort Smith, Arkansas. Please, Mr. McDade, ah, Mark, I'm not bragging. I'm not ashamed of what I have done, yet . . . I understand the gravity of it, and I don't want to be misunderstood."

"Your name is Rebecca?"

"Yes."

"May I call you Becky? I have a little sister by that

171

name. What I now wonder, Becky, is why you found it so necessary to lay this all out for me?"

"Because . . . I find you, ah, most intriguing. You're young, handsome, an American in a foreign land who is obviously doing well. Those are attributes that would make any young woman curious."

"And make your heart pound faster?" Mark teased.

"Don't be ridiculous!" Rebecca snapped. Then she gave him a sly wink. "But it's true, you know. I've been a long time without the company of a cultured gentleman."

Mark stepped closer. Rebecca could smell the heady male scent of him and a slight hint of some essence. Talcum? Or perhaps a cologne. "Tell me that story first. Roger Styles can wait."

"My full name is Rebecca Caldwell Ridgeway," Rebecca began, gathering her resources. "I was widowed two years ago by my own uncle, Ezekial Caldwell. At that time he and Roger were the last of the gang from whom I sought vengeance. After he murdered my husband, we fought. I menaced him with a knife and he fell into a fiery pit of coals. End of story. Roger had escaped me several years earlier, in California. I knew he had come to Mexico, only not to where."

"He's in the state of Guanájuato, on the border with Zacátecas. Using the military governor as a cover, he holds a large *ganadéria*."

"Is that a ranch?" Rebecca asked Mark.

"In a way, yes. They raise fighting bulls. More of that later. Back to your story of being without a gentleman's company."

"I've been living with my father's people, the Red Top Lodge band of the Oglala Sioux."

172

"Good Lord!" Mark blurted. "So that's what accounts for that, ah, almost mystical beauty."

"Thank you, kind sir. Any factors of beauty I may have I attribute to my mother. My father was a craggy, hard-faced Sioux war chief whose scowl would crack an axe head. After Grover's death I was distraught. Uncle Ezekial had also killed my elder stepson. I wanted to die with them, I think. But I had another son, Joey Ridgeway. *Pinzpinzala* he's called now, no—that's not accurate. He's thirteen and had his vision dream. Sharp Eye is his name now, and except for him being tow-headed and blue-eyed, he could pass for any Oglala boy."

"That may be. But you certainly could not pass for *any* Sioux girl. I worked the mines in the Black Hills and I know," Mark assured her.

"Flattery?" Rebecca teased.

"If I need it, yes. Now, the reason I stopped by where you sat was that I could stand it no longer. I had to make your acquaintance and ask you to dine with me at Vanégas. I know just the place."

Rebecca placed a small, warm hand on Mark's shoulder. "Invitation accepted. I'd be delighted to have dinner with you, Mark."

"And you . . . really . . . ah, killed those desperados?" Mark queried hesitantly.

"Do you want me to recount them for you?" Rebecca offered.

"No-no. I think not," Mark hastened to reply.

Rebecca brightened, she glowed, her smile bloomed. "Then I know we'll have a wonderful time, Mark."

Chapter 17

Candlelight made creamy circles on the linen table-cloth. Smiling musicians sang romantic songs of Mexican and Spanish origin in an alcove to one side. The fragile notes of their guitars and light voices quivered in the air. The rich odor of incense blended with the aromas of their just completed meal. Mark McDade wore the expression of a lovesick swain as he took Rebecca Caldwell Ridgeway's hand in his. Over the ten days since Whirlwind's untimely death, Rebecca had been disturbed to discover a reawakening of her normal, healthy urges. She, too, shared a look of love mixed with powerful desire.

"You're more beautiful than ever I've seen you," Mark stated earnestly.

"Thank you, Mark. I'm overwhelmed at the luxury you've shown me here in San Luis Potósi. The truth is I had no idea how people in other lands live. For all my chasing around after Roger Styles, I fear I've remained terribly provincial."

"That's not a crime, you know," Mark countered. "Becky, I . . . I had an ulterior motive in asking you to dinner at this particular place. Most of Mexico lives in the kind of grinding poverty you saw along the tracks.

Only the elite are free to dine in such opulence. I, ah, wanted to dazzle you, impress on you the kind of life we could live. Because," Mark hastened on, to prevent Rebecca from voicing an objection, "I want to convince you to stay here with me."

Anticipating this, though fearing the result, Rebecca still found herself melting inside at the sincerity of Mark's offer. "Mark, oh, Mark, I . . . You've left me quite beside myself," she attempted to frame her rampant thoughts. "I want to stay with you, believe me, I do. You're handsome, successful, sophisticated, and, I suspect, you'd make a marvelous lover. Yet, I must see this through. This may be my last chance to bring Roger Styles to justice. I can't let anything stand in the way of achieving that."

Hurt furrowed Mark's face. "You might not live through it."

"I've . . . always considered that. That's why I never made a promise to come back to anyone. Since my eighteenth year, no make that seventeen and the death of my Oglala husband Four Horns, I have known nothing but violence, death and tragedy. I'd not wish that on anyone. This time . . ." Rebecca paused, swallowed with difficulty, then hurried on, lest she recant. "This time I sense a difference. I *want* to come back. I want to have you for my man, if only for a little while. To do that, I must live. So I will," she ended simply.

"We still have tonight," Mark urged. "And other nights. How soon do you plan to leave?"

"Tomorrow morning," Rebecca answered simply. "We leave for Guanájuato at daybreak."

". . . *lagrimas de peña* . . ." Of a sudden the words of the song had new meaning for Mark McDade. *Tears of sorrow.* His heart filled with them. He found it hard to think clearly, to pursue his careful plan of romance and seduction. He spoke without thinking it through, albeit with acceptance and determination.

"Then I'll go with you. You need someone to watch your back."

"No, Mark!" Rebecca objected vehemently. "There will be too much danger."

"Do you think I've never fought before? That I can't handle a gun, or myself in a battle? Gold and silver mines in Mexico are frequent targets for bandits. I wouldn't be alive today if I consisted of only my, ah, 'sophisticated' side. Say you'll take me. Let me help you. And then . . . then we can explore the future unrestrained. Starting with . . . tonight."

"Oh, Mark, Mark," Rebecca responded in mental turmoil. "I'll neither say yes nor no. If you come it must be of your choosing."

"I've already chosen. So that's settled. Now, as to tonight . . ."

"Yes? Yes, my dear, dear Mark?"

Blue-gray mist in the lower valleys masked the rebels' mountain stronghold from any observer. Secure in their hideout, Xavier Alvarado contemplated what progress had been made so far. True, every time an attempt had been made to confiscate his family holdings, the few troops Ordaz could spare for the task had been driven off. It only forestalled the inevitable, Xavier acknowledged. His lieutenants had made several successful raids.

A look around him verified that. The men ate well, had plenty of clothing and all but a few had firearms, albeit poor ones. They needed more. From Hertado, he had learned of the *segundo*'s special mission. If Pépe Ruiz made a successful trip to *la Capital*, all would be

176

well. Unfortunately, none of the raids so far had been very productive. Ordaz remained in control, as through him, so did Roger Styles. What was needed, Xavier resolved, was a decisive blow against the impudent *gringo*. He stirred himself and started rapidly back to the center of camp.

"Tomás, Umbérto, Curro, come at once," he shouted.

When his officers had assembled, Xavier studied them carefully, then laid out a map of the northern portion of the state. "Here, right on the border with Zacatecas, is the *ganadéria* of Roger Styles. I have decided to seize the initative while Ordaz languishes in San Miguel Allende. Prepare your men. Only the wounded, aged and untrained will remain here. The rest I will lead in an attack on the *gringo's hacienda.*"

A chorus of cheers came from the junior officers. Xavier Alvarado noticed that although he was no less vocal, Tomás Guevera had a cold, calculating glint in his eyes. He pondered his decision regarding Tomás. Had he been rash in reaching the conclusion he had made? A lot of soul searching had gone into the final plans. The fact remained that Xavier did not intend to be gone long. Which made his decision seem less a potential threat.

"Tomás, I am making you camp *comandante*. You and two squads will be in charge of the sick, wounded, women and children. The rest of you prepare your men. We will depart shortly after sundown. The purpose is to set fire to crops and stored grain and burn down the *hacienda* if possible. Take heart, *amigos*. If we carry the day against the *gringo ladrón,* our whole cause may be settled in our favor in a few days' time."

Dust churned up in thick columns from the iron

177

rims of the wagon wheels. Heavily laden with their cargo of six cases of rifles each, ample ammunition, and a decoy cargo above, the wagons from Ciento Leguas rolled along a wide, rutted road northward from Mexico City. Pépe Ruíz felt exceedingly proud, also a good bit relieved.

Much to his surprise, Pépe had taken the letter of authorization to Don Estebán's bank in Mexico City. The manager had been most gracious to him and had arranged for the quantity of gold he had required. This he took to the German.

He had often heard of these mysterious foreign dealers in almost anything. Some took a man's money and never produced the goods, or killed the mark if he made trouble. *Corónel* von Ritter proved to be an honest man. It let Pépe Ruíz dream of getting the rifles through in time to let him frame Pablo Ordaz in the sights of his own new Mauser. The eight day of their journey had dawned crisp and cool, with a hint of powerful sun later in the day.

Draft animals grumbling, they left San Jose del Rio, Carretero, behind them in the dust. Only a short distance separated them from the state capital, then on to the border and into Guanájuato. Soon they would be home. The day passed uneventfully and Pépe set camp north of the hillside-clinging, mining town of Carrétero. A chill ran along his spine as he recalled the stories of the petrified people, the mummies of Carrétero.

Space being so dear in the hard-rock mountains, the vaults in the above-ground cemetery at Carrétero were rented. When the last of the family died, or someone lost interest in paying for a vault, the body residing there was tipped over the open rear end into a huge natural cavern. The pit contained limestone water and other liquid minerals that seeped into clothing, flesh and bone. Tales of finding grandees still in their Spanish armor had thrilled and chilled Pépe as a boy. In fact, they had scared the stiffness right out of Pépe's pecker on several occasions. Now he was encamped within sight of them, across the valley. *Ay diós mio. Santa María ayudame,* Pépe thought nervously.

Noontime the next day found them across the border into their native state of Guanájuato. No sooner had Pépe ordered the march resumed after the midday meal than a patrol of Coronel Ordaz's bandit-Federales intercepted the caravan.

"Who are you and what is your business on the road?" a fat, arrogant bandit in the uniform of a Federale captain demanded.

"I am called Pépe Ruíz, from the village of Célaya," Pépe lied. "We are hauling pigs of iron and smith's charcoal to the blacksmith there."

"Remove the covers," the obese outlaw roared. "These wagons are to be searched."

Pépe Ruíz had kept himself and his men prepared for something like this since departing Carrétero. Although they traveled in the guise of trusted retainers of some prosperous merchant or *haciendado,* each concealed a pair of revolvers under their white cotton shirts. As the officious lackeys of Pablo Ordaz made for the first wagon, Pépe gave a signal. Forty-five caliber Obregons appeared from all quarters.

A withering blaze of fire drove the bandit-police back. Two men lay dead, scarlet staining their tan uniforms. The others reeled in surprise. Before they could rally, another fusillade from the defenders of the wagons sent them into the rocks. Shouted orders restored their cohesiveness. After a long moment of silence, the Federales opened fire and charged.

179

They met with even more devastating fire as the seven men accompanying Pépe Ruíz opened up with Mauser rifles, hidden, but ready, in the wagon beds. Once more the crooked Federales retreated. Angry words, punctuated by an occasional shot, continued over five minutes. It did not occur to Pépe that this was itself a diversion. The Federales recovered their horses and half their number circled wide to attack from the rear.

Too late, Pépe discovered this tactic. The hills surrounding the trail seemed to swarm with tan uniforms. His men had more targets than they could concentrate upon. With wild yells Ordaz's men closed in. Oblivious to the sound, they failed to hear hoofbeats until a tall, broad-shouldered man in buckskin, wielding a limber *coup* stick of Crow Indian design burst among them, striking at astonished Federales. One, then another, and a third fell, knocked unconscious by the goose egg sized stone in the end of the swishing object. Uttering a Crow war cry, Lone Wolf reversed his field and slashed through again. Behind him now came Rebecca, Mark, and Big Nose.

Although Lone Wolf's mystic endeavors had taken him beyond the point where he had forsaken the use of weapons and would not kill a fellow human, the others endured no such restraint. Rebecca's right hand Smith American belched flame and smoke and a .44 slug split the breastbone of a chubby sergeant. She fired again, matching Big Nose's first round. They hit the same incautious bandit who had raised up to take careful aim at this unexpected relief force.

Their bullets sent him into a grotesque dance of death. Mark McDade accounted for the wild-eyed corporal who thrust upward with his bayonet to disembowel Sila. Three of the remaining Ordaz men

180

suicidally rushed the wagons. Shredded by the heavy bullets from the 11mm Mausers, they flopped and scuffed on the ground until claimed by the Grim Reaper. Then, with the swiftness of its beginning, the vicious firefight ended. Numbing silence filled the defile. A horse snorted, two whinnied to each other. A huddled figure in a tan uniform groaned mightily and gave up his life.

"What . . . what a magnificent surprise!" Pépe Ruíz exclaimed. "I do not know who you might be, but you have saved our worthless lives."

"You did quite well yourselves," Rebecca responded. "Anyone fighting the scum of Pablo Ordaz is someone to side with," she went on.

"Ah. Are you with Xavier Alvarado in the hills?". Pépe inquired.

"No. We weren't aware of anyone by that name. We came to kill Roger Styles."

"Praise all the saints," Pépe shouted. "Would the world was filled with people like you." He introduced himself and they reciprocated. "*Don* Marco, I am acquainted with your name, if not your person. It will please Don Estebán to learn you have joined our cause. I'm on my way to the Alvarado *ganadéria*. It would please me if you were to accompany us and I might make it known to Don Estebán that he has allies."

"We would be glad to," Rebecca agreed. "First we should work together to dispose of these bodies. We can be thankful none escaped to carry word of what happened."

"Likewise," Pépe added, "any news of our imminent arrival." He looked about him. "The cost has been high. There are only three of my men left able to fight, with two wounded to ride the wagons. If you would be so kind as to escort us to Ciento Leguas I'll inform the

181

Patrón of your great service. If you prefer to proceed directly to the stronghold, you must follow these instructions precisely." Quickly he gave directions for locating Xavier's stronghold.

With no better plan to offer, Rebecca readily agreed to see the wagons safely through to the *hacienda*. At last they would have a good chance at Roger Styles.

In half an hour the sun would be in the defenders' eyes. Xavier Alvarado had chosen a dawn attack for that purpose. His men, numbering some seventy-five, crouched at the ready in a shallow ravine that ran an irregular course from north to south a scant hundred yards from the *hacienda* at Las Piedras *ganadéria*. They had moved into position during darkness. When the attack came, one third their number would remain behind to provide covering fire, while the remaining fifty would charge. The cluster of outbuildings would be set afire, then the walls assaulted. Xavier well recalled the three foot thick walls, narrow slit windows.

"Would that we had some artillery," he murmured to Umberto at his side.

"De veras, Xavier, that would make this easy." A frown creased Umberto's brow. "We'll lose a lot of men in this."

"Only to gain many more, is my hope, *compañero,"* Xavier responded. "We'll wait until the sun is fully up."

Umberto grunted in satisfaction. "Let them stare into that. We'll be all over them before they know what happened."

"Remember, no one is to load a cartridge into the chamber or cap a nipple until we reach the outbuildings. I don't want any stray shot alerting the *gringo*'s guards," Xavier stressed.

Sharp and brassy, the sun sat the low hills to the east of Las Piedras when fifty men rose from the ravine and ran the short distance in among the clustered structures. Quickly they lighted torches and began to fire the buildings. As each man finished with his task, he paused to load his weapon. A single alarmed voice cried out, then several took up the call.

"Fire! The granary is on fire!"

"The blacksmith's shop is burning."

"Soldiers! There are strange troops here."

Shots began to crackle. Inside the *hacienda,* Roger Styles awakened with a start. He heard the shouts and had his trousers on by the time the first rounds were fired.

"Get the sharpshooters to the roof parapet," he commanded.

Heavily armed men trudged up the sandstone steps to the low, flat platform that ringed the false front of the roofline. At first they saw no one to take aim upon. Then figures began to scurry between the buildings. A moment after they opened up, bullets cracked through the air around them.

"Out there. In the ravine. They have us rang—" the observant sharpshooter's words cut off in a spray of pink froth as a heavy slug pulped his head. From below, the strident voice of Xavier Alvarado directed his troops.

"Shoot the cattle, the horses we can't take, kill anyone who shows his face."

For twenty minutes the battle favored the attackers. Gradually the small, surprised garrison rallied. Reinforced nearly by the minute, their superior volume of firepower started taking an awful toll. Casualties mounted. Although great damage had been done, with a number of torches smashing into the second floor windows of the *hacienda* and starting fires, the terrible attrition struck at Xavier's resolve. A quick count of the battle ground indicated he'd lost at least twenty men.

"There are more than we counted on," he argued aloud to his senior sergeant. "Pass the word to gather up what supplies, weapons and horses we can handle and begin to withdraw." For the hundredth time Xavier Alvarado wished he had the reliable and inventive Paco Alvarez with him.

More men died in the scrambling retreat from the *hacienda*. The survivors covered half a mile before Xavier realized no immediate pursuit threatened them. Unknown to him, Roger Styles had been thoroughly frightened to the extent he would not leave himself vulnerable to a counter-attack by sending his personal guards after the rebels. Only after light patrols ascertained that the field of combat had been cleared of all attackers did Roger authorize a detail to follow his enemy.

Fortunately there were enough horses for the wounded, Xavier thought gratefully. Slowed to a walking gait, the remains of Xavier's valiant band moved slowly toward the mountains. Twice they were compelled to turn and fight holding actions when their pursuers drew too near. By midafternoon, three of the wounded had died. The sanctuary of the mountains seemed no closer than from the start. Sunset still found them exposed on the meadow-like savannah.

"Keep moving. Don't slow down now. Push on," Xavier urged his flagging troops. "We can slip away in the dark."

Through the night they bore on. The column got divided at one point and Xavier feared the worst, until the stragglers caught up. They walked and rested, zigged and zagged while the moon crossed the sky. The greater the distance they put between Las Piedras and themselves, the more encouraged the men became. Then, in that indistinct, gray moment of first light, dark figures appeared athwart their line of march.

Fat and orange, a slice of the sun pushed above the Sierra Madre Occidentál. Increased illumination identified the grim presence as a platoon of Lancers. Xavier's heart pounded in a chest gone hollow. The end, he knew too well, would come swiftly.

"We'll stand and fight where we are," he informed the survivors. "These are Lancéros. Shoot for their horses. They're not too effective without them."

A rider, gaudy in Lancer uniform, detached himself from the center of the line and rode forward. "Do you wish to meet and discuss terms?"

"What terms would be honored by the likes of Ordaz and the *gringo*, Styles?" Xavier asked bitterly.

"If we are compelled to attack, there will be no quarter," the envoy stated flatly.

"I am aware of that," Xavier responded.

From behind the Lancer emissary another man, short, thin, saturninely dark, kneed his horse forward. "Wait a minute. Is . . . is that you, *Teniente* Alvarado?"

Disbelief dizzied Xavier's mind. "Al-Alvarez? Sergeant Paco Alvarez?" Xavier inquired, still not accepting it.

"It's lieutenant now, still all the same it is I. And in charge of this patrol." The diminutive former sergeant trotted forward. His eyes twinkled. "In light of your superior number, and tactical ability, I find myself compelled to yield the field to you, *Señor.*"

"Wha—" Xavier choked out.

"Concern for the well-being of my troops forces me to surrender," Alvarez phrased it differently.

A stunned moment passed. Xavier rode close to his

former sergeant and they exchanged an enthusiastic *abrazzó*. "Under such circumstances, old friend, I can gladly grant quarter. Your men can retrieve their arms at the river crossing."

"No-no-no, *mi-ah-Capitan*," Alvarez protested, noting the makeshift badge of rank on Xavier's epaulets. "We, ah, I had in mind our joining you. I heard of your father's murder, naturally. It was the doing of that *gringo cabrón*. And I have in mind how Ordaz betrayed his most trusted friend, Guevera. After the men began to slip away, I took care in those who replaced them. What do you say, *compañeros?*" Alvarez shouted, rising in his stirrups. "Shall we join the valiant *Capitan* Alvarado and crush the tyrant?"

Shouts of approval came from every throat. When the accolade died out, Xavier grew serious. "You know word of this will get back to Ordaz."

Alvarez shrugged. "Of course. *No es importa*. We are with you to the man."

Chapter 18

". . . Mary, full of Grace, the Lord is with thee. Blessed art thou among women and blessed is the fruit of thy womb, Jesus. Holy Mary, Mother of God . . ."

Crushed by the news of Don Estebán's murder, Pépe Ruíz had become incapable of decisive action. He spent the entire day in the small church, barefoot, dressed in a peasant's white cotton shirt and trousers, instead of his usual finery. His knees on the hard flagstones before a large bank of candles and a statue of the Virgin, he had lighted a large votive and clutched a battered straw hat in his hands, fervently pressed to his breast. Over and over he had prayed the rosary, while tears streamed down his face. Pépe had loved the *Patrón* like a father-savior figure and grew desolate in his overpowering grief. Padre Ignacius despaired for his reason. For the others, life went on.

Saddened, but all the more willing to aid the son after the father's betrayal, Rebecca and her entourage made arrangements to head directly to the mountains. They verified the route and the passwords and started off early the next morning. Pépe remained behind, still praying.

High into the mountains of south-central Guanájuato, Rebecca rejoiced to the heady scent of pine resin, flowering laurel and lush grass, crushed by their horses' hoofs. By her estimate they hadn't far to go. The trail led steeply up the side of one buttress, away from the spring-sweet meadow. It rounded a fat curve and Rebecca had time to notice a sharp drop-off that disappeared into mist. The next instant she recorded the hazardous rockslide that narrowed the trail to a dangerous ledge at the edge of the precipice.

The sharp click of a rifle hammer halted them at once. "What are you doing here?" a disembodied voice challenged.

"We came seeking light and freedom," Rebecca answered in Spanish.

"Here you will only find suffering and death," the hidden sentry responded.

"Then we come to die," Rebecca concluded.

Relaxation of tension could be heard in the voice. "Who sent you?"

"Pépe Ruíz. He has returned with guns," Mark McDade supplied in smooth Spanish.

"Dismount and come around the slide. Be careful not to fall," came the final instruction.

Beyond the obstruction, five men waited, roughly dressed, unshaven for the most part, heavily armed. The spokesman designated one to lead the newcomers to the camp. Rebecca and the others followed for a good mile deeper into the folds, rising in altitude another thousand feet. Only an eagle could successfully attack this place, Rebecca considered. They were met by a small, agitated, fiercely intent young man.

"I am Lieutenant Tomás Guevera, Commander of the camp in the absence of *Capitán* Alvarado. You bring us news?"

"Yes, we do," Rebecca replied.

188

"Please. I was asking your leader," Tomás snapped, oblivious to the insult he paid her.

"I *am* the leader," Rebecca shot back with a note of anger.

Tomás looked confused. "How can that be? You are a . . . a *woman.*"

"I'm not prepared to debate that with boy lieutenants. Are we to be welcomed or should we go on our way?"

Slowly a change came over Tomás. He produced an ingratiating smile and bowed, as he gestured to the collection of huts. *"Mi casa es su casa, señorita.* Don Xavier should return within two days. Make yourselves comfortable and we will do all we can to serve your needs."

Rebecca tried on a little charm. "Why, thank you, Lieutenant Guevera. You are most gracious."

"They say Ruíz is back," the escort remarked.

"Oh? This is so? The *segundo,* Pépe Ruíz, has returned from *la Capital?"* Tomás inquired, his mood changing visibly as he spoke.

"Yes, he has. Right now he is grief-stricken over the death of Don Estebán. When he is himself, within a few days, he'll follow us with more recruits and the armaments he obtained," Rebecca informed Guevera.

An odd light glowed in Guevera's eyes. "He has the guns, has he? How many?"

"Twelve cases, with ample ammunition," Rebecca revealed.

"Aaah. And he is coming here?" Tomás queried.

"Yes."

"Raul, Gustávo, Jorge, disarm them," Tomás snapped out rapidly. "They are under arrest as Ordaz spies. See they are securely confined in the cave room with the barred front."

189

"This is ridiculous," Mark McDade protested. "We're allies."

"You are not so clever as to make me believe that, Señor McDade. You are a *gringo*, a capitalist exploiter of the masses. No one would believe you to be on the side of the proletariat. Take them away."

After the surprised prisoners had been led off, Tomás called Ignacio Torreon to his side. "I want you to take out a detail to recover those weapons. It would be beneficial if poor Pépe Ruíz did not survive the liberation of the arms. You, ah, understand what I mean?"

"Of course, Comrade," Torreon responded readily.

"Bueno. Be gone within the hour."

This unexpected bonus portion of his overall plan under way, Tomás turned his thoughts to the prisoners. One in particular. Images of the delightfully curvy body of the *gringa* who pretended to be their leader rose in Tomás' mind. Her pert breasts, sweet, heart-shaped face, nicely rounded behind, and long legs filled him with the heat of raw lust. His loins stirred and his phallus rose in eager response.

A thin orange-red sliver rested on the western horizon and the rebel camp had become quiet. Broken rock crunched under the boots of two men who came to the confinement cell and peered inside. One lighted a kerosene lantern and held it high.

"Ah, there she is. You, the pretty one, come out here."

"What do you want with me?" Rebecca demanded.

"You are to be questioned by *el Comandanté Priméro,*" the ugly-faced man in tattered uniform coat informed her. His companion snickered.

"Wh-who is that?" Rebecca asked.

190

"He used to be *Teniente* Guevera. Now he has declared the people's revolution and taken his true place as *Comandanté Priméro.* Come along."

Tomás had other things in mind than an interrogation. When his trusted guards brought Rebecca to his quarters, he let his gaze rove over her, savoring the line and form of her healthy, athletic body. When she said nothing and remained unmoving near the door, he crossed to her. One hand lashed out and closed on the bodice of her blouse.

With a hard yank, he tore the cloth away. His eyes bugged at sight of her pert, firm, up-thrust breasts. His mouth went dry, then started to tingle as he began to salivate. He moved closer and began to fondle her. Rebecca had endured all of that she could tolerate at the hands of Roger Styles' bully-boys. Forcing a smile, she stepped back slightly and assayed the bulge at Tomás' crotch.

Well aimed, her knee made solid connection with Tomás' scrotum. He howled with agony and his exquisite erection wilted. Rebecca flayed his cheeks with sharp fingernails. Tomás involuntarily stepped back and Rebecca delivered a solid kick to the groin.

Tomás doubled over and vomited. Reckless of her safety, uncaring about any punishment she might bring on herself, Rebecca slammed her clasped hands into the back of his neck while ramming upward with a knee. The head of the would-be Marxist rebel made a solid, chunking sound as it rebounded from the violent contact. With a soft groan, Tomás curled up on the dirt floor of his shack in a protective fetal position. Rebecca stepped to the doorway, paused a moment then eased the portal open a crack.

After a long, watchful wait, she stepped out into the starry night. Rebecca made some ten long strides away before the guards who had delivered her caught up to her sides.

"Why are you here? *El Comandanté Priméro* had, ah, many things on his mind. He should not be finished with you so soon."

"I'm quite sure *El Comandanté Priméro* got all he wanted from me. More actually. You heard the sounds?" Rebecca asked, thinking quickly.

"Oh, yes."

"He bent me to his will and we, ah, reached a meeting of the minds, you might say. Now he is tired from the questioning and wishes to sleep. You will see me to my accommodations, *cabàlleros?*"

"Most gladly, *señoríta*. If one can so quickly please *Comandanté Priméro*, might another aspire to, ah, great heights also, eh?"

"That, my friends, is for later. Tomorrow night, perhaps?"

Laughter and excited voices awakened the prisoners long after midnight. Cries of surprise blended with other voices. Fires flickered to brightness. Recalling the interest Tomás had in the weapons bring brought by Pépe Ruíz, Rebecca feared the strange bandit might have succeeded in obtaining them.

"Consider one thing. If he's drunk on power, and armed to go on his crazy crusade," Mark McDade suggested, "he'll probably forget about you and what you did to him."

Rebecca considered the condition of Tomás' genitals. "Not too likely, Mark. I hurt him where it hurts most. If anything, he might demonstrate the use of the new rifles by putting me in front of a firing squad."

Laughing, lightly talking men approached the cage.

192

The rusty lock screeched and clicked open. The door flung outward. In the light of a crescent moon, a handsome young man stood hip-shot, arms akimbo. He motioned the light forward and his men spilled into the room. Hat raked back on his well-shaped head, he studied the prisoners.

"I am Captain Xavier Alvarado. It seems I made a most timely early return to our stronghold."

"You — you know about Tomás Guevera?" Rebecca blurted.

"Oh, yes. An old woman loyal to me slipped out of camp and came to advise me of what Tomás had working. After our close call at Las Piedras, and the fortunate acquisition of thirty reinforcements, I decided on a forced march. I must admit her tale made me furious. Come, give me your names and the story of why you are here, then we'll refresh ourselves with *cabrito* and beans and tortillas, drink some beer and I'll explain everything."

After the introductions, the former prisoners were led down to a large cookfire where the carcasses of three goats turned on spits. Cauldrons of beans bubbled, and women patted out the thin corn cakes, to be cooked on a flat iron sheet over a bed of coals. In the midst of the festivities, Rebecca asked Xavier a probing question.

"Where is Tomás Guevera now?"

"He is in his quarters, contemplating the errors of his ways. I always sensed something . . . not quite right about him. I never suspected such sedition. The way I hear it, he planned to obtain the modern firearms, then murder me on my return. Tomás could lead men, but he would never have brought that off. Now, tell me what happened to you."

Rebecca, Mark and Lone Wolf fleshed out the story

193

of their journey to the stronghold, their arrest and confinement. Xavier shook his head sadly at each new revelation. At the conclusion, Xavier came to his feet and waved an arm over them.

"You are of course all free. You may go or stay to fight with me as you see fit. As to Tomás and those who willingly followed him . . ." he paused a moment. Then he summoned his closest aides.

"Gather them up," Xavier commanded. "Put them in the cage where they had these good people confined. We'll put them on trial. Then we shall shoot them. More important, though, is to save those rifles. Paco, select a detail of twenty men. You will command the stronghold, while at dawn the rest of us will ride swiftly to see that Pépe Ruíz and the rifles are made safe and brought here. Now, with the help of the lovely *Señoríta* Rebecca, we will eat and drink and celebrate our double victory."

Three hundred men, all in part or full uniform as Federales, gathered in the plaza outside the *hacienda* at Las Piedras. Storm clouds of anger gathered in Roger Styles' slate-gray eyes and he paced about his study in a jerky manner that betrayed his barely controlled fury. He repeatedly clasped and unclasped his hands, as though wringing the neck of someone he implacably hated. Pablo Ordaz and five subordinate officers stood waiting for Roger to return to the matter at hand.

"We are going to go on the offensive with a vengeance," Roger grated out. "We will strike and keep on striking, until there is not a one of these vermin left alive. They attacked *me*. They attacked Las Piedras, killed fifteen men and burned down everything except the church and the *hacienda*. Spies have informed me of the whereabouts of this stronghold. It shall be up to you to wipe it from the face of the earth."

"We have artillery now, Don Roger. Three six pound gallopers we, ah, liberated from the barracks of the deceitful Lanceros."

"What is this?"

Immediately uncomfortable with the realization Roger did not know of the defection of the Lancers, Ordaz stammered his reply. "The, ah, Lancers have, er, deserted their post, Don Roger. They are, ah, b-believed to have, ah, gone ov-over to the, er-ah, rebels."

"Sons of bitches!" Roger howled. "Are all Mexicans cowards and turncoats?"

"We are loyal, Don Roger," Hector Blancos protested. "All of us are loyal to *Presidente* Diáz. And, because of it, to you. Count on us."

Ordaz gave him a dark look. Could it be Blancos schemed to replace him? "We are ready to take to the field. I have three hundred men. Also, the three remaining platoons of Lancers have not fled their posts. They are on the way here and will rendezvous with us at the headwaters of the Rio Querál in the foothills."

"Good. I want you to detach fifty men to ride to Ciento Leguas. They are to arrest all the women and children, burn the villages and the ranch buildings to the ground. Spare the *hacienda*, only because I think it would make a nice new home for you. Provided," Roger added with a meaningful pause, "you are successful in this. Now get out of here. All of you. And don't come back until you are victorious."

Chapter 19

Crystal clear and frightfully cold, the little stream that meandered from its hidden spring through the rebel camp made musical gurgles and trills that enchanted the children. Although far too cold for swimming, they would sit on the gravel bank and dab their feet in the water until it began to hurt. Left behind with her friends to strengthen the hand of Paco Alvarez, Rebecca savored the respite. Xavier had placed the former sergeant in charge of these less than reliable followers and the prisoners. If any prisoner attempted to escape, or should an effort be made by the doubtful patriots to deliver them from confinement, Alvarez was ordered to shoot to kill all of those involved. Despite this knowledge, Rebecca managed to enjoy her look at a rebel camp in Mexico.

She had been assured that this one was quite typical. Located in a steep canyon with only a single easily guarded access, the camp housed the fighting men, their women and children. With such hostages to fortune, Rebecca wondered how could the men ever become efficient soldiers. With Xavier and his main force gone, the daily routine resembled more a market square, with housewives haggling over the price of fish or beans. Preparation of the typical Mexican dishes, she observed, seemed to take nearly all of a woman's time. Camp chores and lazy activity were interrupted by three rifle shots from a distant sentry.

"There's some extreme danger," Paco Alvarez informed the newcomers.

A rider thundered in from the outpost at the rock slide, froth foaming his horse's mouth. "Word has come from below, *Jéfe*," he shouted to Alvarez. "There is a regular army approaching. They have cannon, three of them, and the men to work them."

"They'll not get those up the narrow trail," Alvarez spoke confidently.

"The cannons, and one company of soldiers, have taken the east road," the excited messenger informed his listeners. "It is wider, unguarded, and from that plateau . . ." He pointed across the mist-blanketed gap toward another mountain. "They can fire directly into camp."

Suddenly the secure little haven, with its creek and hidden spring, and narrow approach became a trap. It would take too long to evacuate everyone by the steep, hazardous climb along the back wall. While Alvarez pondered this change in circumstances, Lone Wolf came to Rebecca at a trot. He led her palouse stallion, Sila, already saddled, with weapons in place. Around them, frantic women tried to gather up excited offspring and take them further back in the canyon for at least partial safety.

"You must ride like the wind. Go to Xavier to warn him that his stronghold is under siege."

"Yes. But I had thought that someone else might," Rebecca hesitated, not wanting to seem to abandon the cause.

"You are light, Sila is strong. Of anyone, you have

197

the best chance," Lone Wolf reasoned.

Her reluctance banished, Rebecca swung into the saddle and heeled Sila into a quick trot. Clear of the camp she increased her gait to a fast canter, conscious for the first time that Lone Wolf and Big Nose thundered after her. They halted at the sentry post to swell the defenses, while Rebecca rode on at a gallop, once past the rock slide. A mile down the canyon, a flicker of movement caught her attention.

"What's that, Sila?" she asked calmingly.

Her keen eyes soon picked out squat bronze figures with huge chests and long legs, bulging with enormous muscles. She flashed past several of the Tiajumara scouts before they reacted to her presence. One jumped into the road and raised a short, powerful bow. Rebecca, a Smith American ready in her hand, shot him through the chest.

He fell away and she loosed two more rounds in the direction of the thin screen of harriers. Her hurried departure had been none too soon, Rebecca discovered as she rounded another twist and encountered the mounted vanguard of the Federales. Her unexpected appearance gave them pause long enough for her to race forward, bowling two horses and their riders from her path with Sila's broad chest.

One quick-thinking Federale made a grab for her, only to be blasted into eternity with a .44 round from the smoking Smith and Wesson Rebecca aimed at his face. Clear of the confused men, Rebecca urged more speed. Bullets cracked past close to her head and she heard the reports of rifles. A disorganized pursuit of sorts formed and a glance backward showed their grim faces. Rebecca gnawed at her lower lip and drummed her heels into Sila's flanks.

With no more weight than Rebecca aboard, the

mighty palouse stallion began to open his lead. Another hot slug grazed her hat and sent it flying.

Pépe Ruíz selected a campsite for the night somewhat early and with considerable trepidation. At first he had been relieved when reinforcements arrived. Tomás, he had been told, sent them because he felt there might be need of greater strength. As the day wore on, something in their attitude, like they shared a joke to which he was not privy, began to make him nervous. He had hoped and expected that Xavier would arrive with enough men that he could break open the crates and proceed as an armed band, too powerful to challenge. When, at the midday meal, Ignácio had demanded he do just that, Pépe had demurred on the grounds that it would make them too conspicuous if they carried fine new rifles. He pointed out that they would still be too few to defend the wagons. Or, for that matter, to carry off all the rifles if attacked. Even when he had prevailed upon Ignácio to ride at a distance from the wagons, lest the presence of the rough-looking men attract the attention of Federale patrols to the rifles, his unease had not lessened.

Ingácio Torréon reluctantly agreed and took his men forward a hundred yards. Once out of earshot, he revealed his new plan to his second in command. "Oscar, we will play along with this old fool until the time is right. Then I shall personally kill him. We will also kill any of his followers who will not swear allegiance to *Comandanté Priméro* Guevera and our cause."

Torréon considered the night camp an ideal occasion for his nefarious scheme. During the afternoon he had refined it somewhat, so that he held off while the evening meal was prepared and eaten and the routine

199

chores attended to. Pépe had also been considering the course of events and exhibited no surprise when he found himself the focus of the traitors' guns.

Chris Starret hated admitting failure. He hated even more the prospects his future might hold after reporting to Roger Styles. After a fruitless search in Nebraska, then later Texas, he had at last given up and brought his three surviving men, Jim Elkhorn, Hank Bridger and Harry Gonzales-Gonzales south to Las Piedras. They arrived after the great campaign had been launched and rode two days to catch up. Surprisingly Roger seemed little disturbed at their empty-handed return.

"She's an elusive bitch, no denying it," Roger passed off the lack of success. "The important thing is that you're back here in time to help smash the last vestige of resistance in this portion of Mexico. Before long we shall enter Mexico City in triumph, the emperor and his new aristocracy."

Chris had no doubt as whom Roger saw as emperor. In light of that, he wanted to change the subject. "That Rebecca and her companions kept moving southward. We lost track of them way down in Texas, near Laredo. My bet would have been that she headed right here to find you."

"Only there's been no sign of her. Dismiss Rebecca Caldwell from your worries, Chris. The lead elements of this little army have made contact with the rebels. In the morning we'll have a fine little fight and exterminate them like vermin."

"You are a symbol of the capitalists who are destroying our country," Ignacio shouted at the bound figure of Pépe Ruíz.

Trussed like a pig for the slaughter, Pépe Ruíz lay near the fire. His men had been disarmed and stood in a surly knot. Ignacio had been haranguing them for half an hour, extolling the supposed virtues of some impossible sounding political-economic system. Now he appeared to have reached the purpose for all of it.

"These men who follow you are workers and peasants. They, like us, will become the inheritors of the Brave New World. You, Pépe Ruíz, may have come from the masses, but you are a lackey of the oppressors and for you there is no hope. That is why I must execute you now, in the name of the revolution."

Sweat beads popped out on Pépe's forehead and he squeezed his eyelids tightly shut. Half-remembered prayers tumbled through his brain. He tensed at the distinctive clicks of an Obregon hammer. He had only seconds to live.

Odd, he thought a moment later. One isn't supposed to hear the shot that kills them. He still felt the chill of impending death, the heat of the campfire on his face, rough ground beneath his back. Tentatively he opened his eyes. A blue-edged, red-washed black hole had appeared on Ignacio's forehead. His eyes bulged in their sockets and blood ran from his nose and ears. Pépe needed no close examination to know the back of the rebel traitor's head had been blown away.

Exclamations of surprise and anger came from Torréon's followers. Pépe heard the scrape of boot soles on the hard ground and blinked to clear his vision. Xavier and five of his trusted aides entered the ring of firelight. One held a smoking rifle.

"Such scum as this should not be given a proper burial. Let the wolves have him," Xavier stated flatly.

201

Gratitude and affection overflowed Pépe's heart.

"Untie him," Xavier commanded. Then he personally helped the old *segundo* to his feet and embraced him in effusive manly fashion. "We nearly lost you, old friend. If it hadn't been for the young lady you sent my way, we would have never known about the rifles or of the treachery that threatened. I've confined Tomás and his supporters at the camp. These new rifles will certainly be an advantage when we go after Ordaz and his rabble. First, though, we must return to the canyon and rally all the men."

With a banshee shriek, a six pound projectile arced through the twilight and landed with a thunderous explosion near a cookfire pit. Chunks of ground and slivers of iron whistled through the air. The women and children had withdrawn as great a distance as possible. It didn't eliminate the danger though. Several men had been wounded, and Mark McDade now commanded the rear guard. Down at the barricade, Lone Wolf and Big Nose fought with Paco Alvarez and five men to hold the Federales of Ordaz's command on the far side of the rock slide. Before the sun had set, Lone Wolf took a count of bodies and dead horses that littered the slope and trail.

Ordaz seemed indifferent to spending the lives of his mounted troops in an effort to breech the major defense of the canyon. While he did so, Lone Wolf wondered, what was Ordaz doing with his infantry? The air rippled again to the sound of a passing shot.

In the camp another of the defenders lost the unfair contest to a cannon ball. Several others had given up their lives in the same manner, four more at the slide. If the infantry somehow gained an advantage, they would be pushed back and slaughtered like rabbits in a net drive, Lone Wolf realized. Without those cannon, the battle would be a lot more even.

"We need to put those cannon out of commission," Lone Wolf observed to Paco.

"True, but how?"

"If we can hold out until full darkness we might have a chance for a small expedition to make a foray and spike the guns."

"For a man who will not kill," Paco remarked to Lone Wolf, "you sure know a lot about warfare."

Lone Wolf grinned ruefully. "Purely by absorption. I was a drummer boy, a lad of thirteen, in an Ohio regiment during our Civil War."

"We learned the technique of spiking guns in the Lancers," Paco advanced. "If you think this will work, choose from among my Lancers and when it is dark we'll give it a try."

Lone Wolf returned to camp to search out materials. It proved of little difficulty since one of the rebels was a blacksmith and had brought along the tools of his trade. Like a monotonous metronome, the enemy continued to lob shells into camp. Whimpers of fear and the sobbing of terrified children came from far too close. Lone Wolf hardened himself to the sound and set about selecting volunteers.

Chapter 20

Wrapped in an envelope of silence, with darkness falling, Rebecca paused to study her backtrail. So far as she knew, she had lost her pursuers, except for a pair of Tiahumara Indians. They were the least of her worries. She didn't know the country, nor the exact whereabouts of Xavier's main force. She dare not stop to rest her tired stallion. Legendary runners, the Tiahumara Indians could have easily kept pace with her all through the waning afternoon.

For certain they would still be able to move faster than her worn out animal, despite the cool breeze that appeared to freshen him. Sila put his head down and cropped a large tuft of lush, green grass. With a tired little sigh, Rebecca kneed the palouse into motion and continued to pick her way along narrow, boulder-strewn road in the near total darkness before moonrise. A tiny premonition nagged at the back of her consciousness.

Armed with only a knife and the two heavy Smith & Wesson No. 4s in her pommel holsters, her nervous mental prodding prompted Rebecca to draw the razor-sharp little skinning knife from her belt sheath and conceal it in her lap. She held it with the blade against her right wrist, the reins in her left hand. This accomplished, she urged a drooping-headed Sila on at a slow walk. The only warning she had was a flicker of Sila's ears.

An instant later, the stallion jerked his head back with a Tiahumara on the bit. Another leaped to drag Rebecca from the saddle. With screams of pure animal ferocity from both horse and rider, Rebecca sank the little knife in the chest of her attacker. She managed to jerk it crosswise before it rippled from her hand, slippery with gushing blood. Partly yanked from the saddle, she succeeded in a grab for the horn. She scrabbled left-handed for a huge horse pistol while she pulled upright.

Her world lurched as the stallion hunkered down and scuffled backward, dragging the other Tiahumara. The savage released the bit to lunge for Rebecca, which freed Sila's head to move as the valiant horse willed. The pistol in her hand at an awkward angle, Rebecca could not reach the hammer. She ran out of time to shift her grip as she came face to face with the Indian scout whose hand gripped vise-like at her throat in an attempt to drag her from the stallion's other side. Abruptly there came an ear-shattering shriek as the Indian released her and fell away.

He doubled up in agony as Sila's teeth came together through the loose skin of his side. Fire washed the temple of the Tiahumara warrior's head, illuminating the gaping hole where Becky's bullet passed through his skull. Startled, Sila released his victim and bolted back up the trail in the wrong direction. Rebecca clung desperately, again only half in the saddle, and frantic lest the animal slam into any one of a hundred hazards.

"Whoa, Sila, whoa, boy," she cooed to him in Lakota. "Easy, boy, easy now."

Eventually Rebecca managed to halt the trembling animal. Then, with wobbly knees, she screwed up her courage and led the skittish animal back through the battlefield. By then the moon had risen and bathed the ground in milky light. It gave an eerie effect to the corpses, which Rebecca was relieved to see remained in place. More than a little edgy herself, she wended her way between them, trying to keep both in sight at once. Too tired to do more than jerk his head at the smell of gore, Sila followed with rippling skin. Slowly her confidence returned and Rebecca realized that if she were to reach Xavier, she must lead Sila quite a distance farther.

By the time she gained a hundred yards from her unsettling encounter, she had a spring in her step and a wild sense of elation took hold. If it weren't so dangerous, she would burst into song, she thought with giddy relief, then wondered why a brush with death invariably had this effect.

Fortunately the moon would rise late, Lone Wolf thought as he led a party of ten volunteers down the steep incline from the stronghold. Big Nose and Paco Alvarez had insisted on accompanying the spiking detail and Lone Wolf heartily approved. They had a considerable distance to travel, most of it up or down hill. To cover their movement, they followed along the stream bed for as far as they could. Lone Wolf built a solid respect for the ability of the men to move quietly. Not quite as good as a Crow war party, but enough for their purpose. He estimated some twenty minutes had passed when they started the grueling upgrade to the small plateau where the three cannon sat.

Their way impeded now by increasing underbrush,

206

Lone Wolf caught himself holding his breath, waiting for the scrape and crunch of a betraying blunder. Less than three hundred yards separated them from the lip of the plateau. Any sound now would put them at the mercy of the gun crews. A bright orange flash and terrible blast announced another of the periodic shots from the battery.

Would the crews never go to sleep? Another hundred yards and they would be in full sight of the gunners. Lone Wolf signaled his men to the ground, then crawled to a youth of seventeen, to whisper his revised plan.

"At least one crew is alert. We must go around them and come from behind," Lone Wolf explained to Céasar Ortega, who spoke fair English. "Tell the others to follow me to the south along the curve of the ground. This will take longer, but it should work."

"We will take them by surprise?" Céasar inquired.

"We had better," Lone Wolf told him tersely. "Pass the word. We'll move out at once."

He rejoined Big Nose and started off. The veteran warrior recognized the stratagem without needing instructions. He advanced on hands and knees behind Lone Wolf until they reached a point beyond a curve that would hide their arrival on the top of the plateau. The former Crow warrior pointed upward and started to climb.

When the tense party assembled on the top, each man unsheathed his knife. Two, Lone Wolf noted, had brought machetes. He, Alvarez and the youthful Ortega would tend to the spiking of the touch holes. If luck held and they had the time, Paco had suggested ramming a ball down each tube into the chamber area. It would cause further delay in ever firing the guns again. Through his interpreter, Lone Wolf explained the next step.

"Take the ones who are up and moving first. Sleeping men can't do any harm. Be careful, quick and sure. Leave none of them alive."

Lone Wolf experienced a strain beyond any the others might suffer. Even commanding such an endeavor diminished his spirit self. It would require long hours of purification and prayer to restore the balance of his nature. Yet this task must be performed, he accepted. With a final word of encouragement, Lone Wolf led the way.

Corporal Níeto heard a soft crunch of gravel a moment before the machete blade flashed in the starlight and struck his head from his shoulders. His undirected body did a frightening dance while the severed arteries fountained scarlet into the night. Around him, the members of his gun crew also met swift and violent ends. Silence prevailed while ten men advanced on others of the battery. The eleventh strode to the closest cannon.

Five more cannoneers died in their sleep before any disturbance aroused the unsuspecting soldiers. A shout of alarm turned to a gurgling hiss when one artilleymen awakened a moment before his assailant slit his throat. Two others awakened, only to have their skulls split, crown to chin, with machetes. Metal rang on metal as the remaining three troopers perished in sleep-drugged panic.

Carefully Lone Wolf fitted the hardened iron nail into the touch hole and drove it down with solid blows of his hammer. Spiking cannon could not be done silently. The distinctive tintinabulation echoed down the canyon. When the spike could be driven no more,

Lone Wolf set to breaking it off. The smoother the surface, the less the chance the gun would ever fire again. Another clanging started as Céasar Ortega began his work. Paco Alvarez seated his tapered nail and slammed it solidly. A regular anvil chorus resounded from the mountains.

At the distant camp of mounted troops, the distinctive sound of the spiking operation alerted the sentinels, who roused the Lancers. Quickly they saddled, mounted and sped off along the winding track that led to the plateau.

Lone Wolf heard the approaching horsemen first. Hampered by darkness, he believed them to be a minimal threat. Then he saw the red-orange flickers through the screening trees. To both flanks of the approaching skirmishers riders in single file held torches high above their heads. An idea flickered at the edge of his consciousness.

"Blow their powder supply," he called out.

Quickly Paco and Céasar complied. Lone Wolf spilled loose grains from an open barrel over the stack of kegs set at a distance from his cannon. He fashioned an explosive charge from an empty wine bottle, inserted a length of cannon fuse and built a trail of powder from it toward the lip of the plateau.

"Get to the edge," he called out. "Fire off your powder trains, then everyone over."

Céasar echoed his commands. By then the first of the Lancers broke free of the trees and charged the small detail. Flame crackled from five revolvers and one of Paco Alvarez's men fell dead. Big Nose unslung his Sioux bow and sent arrows on the way with lightning speed. One sank into the chest of a plunging horse. It squawled and bucked, dislodging the rider, and ran back among those not yet deployed off the trail. Another arrow lodged in the shoulder of a Lancer, who howled in pain and pulled rein short of the thin line of defenders. Lone Wolf struck a lucifer and lighted the powder grains on the ground before him.

Quickly he trotted backward, drew his knife and coup stick. Knives and machetes against lances and revolvers could not prevail, he knew.

"Over the side! Hurry!" he shouted.

He turned to follow his own advice and saw Big Nose go down, blood gouting from an ugly exit wound in the big Oglala's back. Lone Wolf dodged a hurtling lance point and scrambled over the edge. Thunderous explosions erupted above. Dirt, metal, wood and bits of Lancers flew high in the night sky. Shaken, weak in the knees, Lone Wolf gathered himself and assembled his small force.

"We've lost three men," he said through Ortega. "We should try to get back the bodies."

"No chance until the soldiers leave," Paco Alvarez informed him. The tough former NCO was gray-faced and he held a brightly colored kerchief to his left shoulder to staunch the flow of blood.

"It's my fault," Lone Wolf stated simply. "We took too much time. A guard should have been posted. Trip lines across the trail. Something . . ." he ended helplessly.

"We'd better start back," Alvarez suggested.

"Yes," Lone Wolf agreed.

Along the way, Lone Wolf sank into deeper gloom. Three men had died because of his plan to spike the guns. Not counting the fifteen artillerymen they had killed, or the ones who died when the powder reserves blew, he reminded himself. Better it had been him. Guilt rose up like a monstrous tide and eroded away his mystic powers. His proximity to violence had been steadily depleting them for several weeks. Yet now Lone Wolf knew he would have to travel a most difficult road to recoup them. At all costs he must avoid any further regression, give up his quest, or take the left hand path.

No, sooner he would take his own life than turn to the left.

Sunrise found Roger Styles in a rage. "How could you let them spike those cannon?" he demanded of the officer in command of the guns. "The Lancers should have been camped with you."

"The cannon fire made their horses nervous," the portly, mustachioed artillery captain replied with a shrug.

"Now we're going to have to go in there and dig them out. With your guns useless, you're now an infantry-man. Organize the men you have left and prepare to lead the attack."

"You do me great honor, Señor." His sarcasm was not lost on Roger.

"Half an hour, Captain," Roger warned darkly.

Thirty minutes later, trumpets flared briefly and the advance set off. Spread along the slope for fifty yards each side of the road, as well as the mounted advance on the rutted trail, the troops strode purposefully, faces grim, movements wooden. Nearing the rock slide barricade, they opened fire on command.

Too many to repulse, or even to delay for long, Paco Alvarez made a quick evaluation. "Pull back," he ordered the defenders.

211

"Widen that spot," Roger commanded when he reached the rubble. Abandoning the advantage of their initial assault's impetus, the soldiers set to clearing away rocks and dirt. They had expanded the space by some five feet when a disturbance began down the road.

First one shot blasted the mid-morning clearness. Then three erupted, followed by a disciplined volley. Perplexed, Roger turned about for some advice or information.

"What's going on?" he demanded.

"We're being attacked in the rear, Excellency," a nervous lieutenant informed Roger. "A large force, well armed."

Battlements had been erected at the lower edge of camp. Armed and determined, the men left for Paco Alvarez to command manned the barricades and kept up a steady fire. Even some of the women wielded rifles alongside their menfolk. Mark joined them. He witnessed the stir of confusion and panic among the enemy and wondered at it. Keen eyed Paco soon had the answer. Jubilant, he rose up to exhort friend and foe alike.

"*Compañeros*, it's Xavier. He is back, with the new rifles and many men. He's attacking the rear. *Lancéros*, abandon the *gringo* and his unjust cause and join your chosen leader. Fight for Alvarado and freedom!"

Hector Blancos had a perfect sight picture. Gently he squeezed the trigger of his rifle. It slammed comfortably against his shoulder and through the quickly dissipating smoke he saw Paco Alvarez lurch. Swaying

212

slightly, the thin ex-sergeant remained upright a moment later, rifle raised above his head. Then he folded in the middle and fell behind the barricade. At once five rifles grew yellow blooms at their muzzles.

Bullets whizzed and cracked around Hector as he ducked for cover. Not fast enough, he discovered as a hot slug removed hair, scalp and a half inch wide trench of bone from the top of his skull. He never knew his lucky shot had come too late.

Stirred by the words of Paco Alvarez, the remaining Lancers whirled their horses and charged through the startled infantry. Lance tips pointed skyward, they raced over open ground to join Xavier's forces. Immediately Xavier ordered an advance.

Chapter 21

Caught between two forces, Roger Styles had no choice but to give battle accordingly. Noon came in a flurry of fighting. The mountain air hung gray and heavy with powder smoke. Men and animals screamed and died. The wounded staggered off if possible to avoid further injury. A third of Xavier's force fought its way through the enemy position and joined the defenders of the stronghold. Bugles sounded the recall and the savaged combatants disengaged.

"First Poppa, now Paco Alvarez," Xavier snarled to his second in command. "I'll take great pleasure boiling that *gringo cabrón* in oil."

"Our *amigos* in the camp are reinforced now. These new Mauser rifles are magnificent. With them we can cut the *gringo*'s men to pieces," Lt. Cervantes enthused.

"We haven't that much time. Our supplies are limited. We must end this by tomorrow midday," Xavier declared.

Eager to fight, the Lancer officers urged another attack. Xavier agreed and the charge sounded once more.

"They're coming again," Chris Starret said needlessly to Roger Styles.

"Yes, damnit. Somehow everything has gone wrong. We need something to turn the battle to our favor."

"You're the bossman, you figure it out," Chris recommended dryly.

The volume of fire increased as the contending forces clashed. It drowned out Roger's angry reply. Wet with sweat, the usually dapper Roger sought desperately for some sign of an opening, a weak point. A man ten feet in front of Roger screamed hideously as a lance point drove clear through his body. Roger snapped off a shot that cleared the Lancer from his saddle, then sprang to the protection of a supply wagon when shouting infantrymen rushed in behind the plunging horse.

Within minutes the opposing armies slugged their way apart. Corpses of men and horses littered the ground. Panting and wearied, tongues lolling from thirst, the fighting men revealed the need for a respite. Reluctantly Xavier ordered a delay. The afternoon stole away and twilight found the opponents stalemated. Cookfires twinkled in all three camps and an apparent truce held while the exhausted troops refreshed themselves.

Xavier watched his men line up to receive a tin plate filled with beans, chorizo sausage and tortillas. Sturdy fare for the hard time they would have on the morrow. His thoughts turned to the lovely and courageous young woman who had brought him news of the siege at such great effort and risk to herself. She had further distinguished herself by selflessly working with the wounded through the bloody fighting of the day. He

215

saw the shadow of her delightful figure now, illuminated on the canvas wall by the kerosene lanterns in the rough field hospital. Compassion, and a touch of something else, stirred in him and Xavier crossed to the crowded entrance.

"*Señorita*," he addressed her. "You have done enough, too much in fact, for one day. Come away with me. I insist you refresh yourself and take a meal with me in my tent."

"But there are more wounded," Rebecca protested.

"Who will be amply cared for by the surgeon's helpers. It's not seemly for a lady of your obvious quality to endure such terrible scenes."

Rebecca washed blood from her hands and brushed back a stray lock of her raven hair. "Oh, believe me, Xavier, I've seen a lot worse. I do thank you for your kindness." She staggered on the uneven ground. "My! I'm a lot more tired than I thought. You wouldn't have some hot tea handy?"

"No, but I do have two bottles of chilled beer. Any one of my men would gladly kill dragons for a single one of them. You may have them both."

"I'll share . . . and gladly," Rebecca answered lightly.

Inside the command tent, Xavier dispatched an orderly for plates of food and opened the beer. "I sent him to the Lancers fire because they have some roasted goat. Chorizo is an acquired taste," he told Rebecca, handing her a damp bottle. "They are only as cool as the stream can make them."

"Ummmm," Rebecca murmured through a long swallow. "That's quite good enough."

"You rested well enough in the wagon?" Xavier prompted.

"Yes, it was easy after my long night. It's fortunate

216

you had come that far. Now we have Roger trapped."

Xavier scowled. "I'm not so certain. If word of this battle reached the wrong people in *la Capital,* we could have a full-sized army fall on us."

"Who would be the right people?" Rebecca prompted.

"My former commander, Colonel Escobar. He is loyal to the president, but he is also wise to Styles and his faction."

Xavier stretched and winced. Then he rubbed at his neck. Noting his apparent discomfort, Rebecca put her beer aside and came to him.

"Is something the matter?"

"Only that I'm stiff and sore. I kept clenching my teeth, shouting, and straining all day."

"Here, let me see if this will help," Rebecca offered, stepping behind him.

With firm and expert hands she began to massage Xavier's neck. He started to relax at once. "Aaah. With this and all your other talents, I should be begging you to marry me," he said lightly. He had not been so at ease in weeks, Xavier realized.

Rebecca continued to knead his stiff muscles. "It's a wonder you don't have a headache fit for two," she observed.

"More like three, truth to tell," he came back. "That's absolutely marvelous. I'd like to order this for all my men. Then we could whip lions tomorrow."

"For now, for just a little while, forget about the fighting," Rebecca urged.

While Rebecca's nimble fingers worked their magic, other forces kindled within her healthy young body. By the time Xavier's eyelids drooped, Rebecca fairly seethed with desire. Her nipples had hardened and she

217

breathed irregularly, while passion made her senses swim. Xavier inhaled her radiated arousal and began to respond. The faint stirring in his groin elongated and swelled into a demanding erection. His heart thudded like an Aztec ceremonial drum. Dry lips demanded attention.

"After we eat . . ." his husky voice suggested.

"No. *Before* we eat. I'll fasten the flaps while you prepare us a place," Rebecca suggested.

They undressed hurriedly. Hunger and fatigue forgotten, they gloried in the revelation of their flesh. Rebecca came to his arms and he embraced her, his rigid manhood burning hotly against her flesh. They kissed, tongues exploring. Rebecca ran her hands down his back to his hard, flat buttocks. Grasping tightly she gyrated her pelvis against his hardened bulk.

"The cot," Xavier whispered.

No matter how ungainly the position might actually appear, Rebecca seemed a vision of divine loveliness as she lay on her back, legs wide-spread to receive Xavier. He came to her in a rush, thrusting deeply as though to consume all in an instant. Rebecca sighed to cut off a squeal of delight. Cares and terrors slid away from them as they swirled off into the temporary eternity of perfect physical joy.

Abruptly the world shifted to a different plane and brightness exploded in Rebecca's head. "D-d-d-on't ever let it end," she keened into Xavier's ear.

Battle lines formed in the dim light of morning. A heavy mist hung in the canyon, bearding the mountain tops around the arena of death. Left out of the fighting by both the dictates of machismo and Xavier's genuine concern for her safety, Rebecca fretted in the surgical tent. Her bold surrender of the previous night tormented her. Across the battlefield, beyond Roger Styles' more than two hundred men, Mark McDade waited for her. Neither had made commitments to the other, yet she felt in the chill of dawn, that she had somehow wronged him.

Her body had always betrayed her. Or rather, as she preferred it, led her to great pleasure.

Xavier wanted her, not only her eager and willing body, but her personality and presence. She knew it, though he had spoken but lightly about it. Mark wanted her too. Her trouble was that she wanted them both. Over the years of her quest there had been many men. And a few boys, she admitted with inner embarrassment. Though they had proven themselves men enough once their bodies joined with hers. Reckless? No. Greedy? Certainly not. She had always given equally, or more. Crisp bugle notes intruded on her reflections and drew her to the grim present, as they summoned the fighting men to their stations.

Unexpectedly, a distant clarion answered. Rebecca came to her feet, her unresolved self-examination abandoned. What could it mean? An outpost messenger thundered into camp as she came from the tent.

"Captain Alvarado!" he shouted. "There's a whole army coming. Fully seven hundred. *Por dios,* they have cannon and mortars, long lines of infantry."

"Do you recognize them?" Xavier asked anxiously.

"No. They will be here soon. Then you shall know," he offered fatalistically.

In ten minutes, during which Xavier and his junior officers worried silently over the outcome, the long

219

column came into view. Unable to stand fast and await his fate like a stoic, Xavier mounted his horse and trotted out. At a hundred yards he began to smile. At fifty he waved and shouted back to his men.

"It's all right. Everything is fine."

Coronel Carlos San Antonio María Escobar de Nuñez greeted Xavier with a huge *abrazzó* and a bellow of good natured chiding. "Had to wait it out and let me save you, eh? What sort of officers have I been bringing up of late? Come, man, where is this mighty battle being fought here that I heard of?"

"If you are that eager, my dear Colonel, let me lead you to the front lines," Xavier responded.

Escobar sobered. "Word of this reached me two days ago. I had no doubt as to your loyalty so I gathered my forces and we marched. All last night, as a matter of fact, after we left the train. Come, let's smash these scum like we should have months ago, eh?"

"Escobar?" Rober Styles exploded. "That does it. He's wanted Ordaz on a gallows all along. He'll show no mercy. I don't know about the rest of you," he told his personal staff, "but I'm leaving. Chris, you get your boys ready. We'll ride out while we have the chance. Shoot anyone who gets in our way."

"Right, boss. Where do we head?"

Roger thought a moment. "South, toward Carrétero. We must go on to Mexico City and seek protection from *Presidente* Diaz."

Before the first shots in what proved a remarkably short engagement blasted the morning air, Roger and his trusted retainers galloped away, leaving Pablo Ordaz to his fate.

Outnumbered more than four to one, the rag-tag army of Pablo Ordaz fired a few volleys for the sake of honor, then seized their leader and surrendered. Jubilant at so quick and easy a victory, Xavier rode among the bandits and corrupted Federales. At his side, Col. Escobar studied the prisoners and occasionally made a remark to an aide.

"That one . . . and those three. Ordaz's bandits. Separate them from the rest. Over there. Another one. That entire platoon. Mark the regular Federales for prison. The rest we'll hang or shoot."

Xavier winced at the sternness of his old commander's edict. Yet, he couldn't fault him. He had one final goal of his own. "Coronel, with your permission, I would like to put the rope around Pablo Ordaz's neck."

"Granted. I heard of what he did to your father."

"Thank you, sir. And now, when we finish this, would you accept the more comfortable facilities of my, ah, stronghold?"

"Gladly. And then I want to hear all that has occurred up here," the old officer requested.

Xavier called for his horse and also for Rebecca to accompany them, introducing her to Col. Escobar. Chatting politely about unrelated matters, they trotted past the barricades and into camp. The party reined up at the stone building Xavier used as a headquarters. As they dismounted, a sudden, lightning movement stunned them to immobility.

Snarling with rage, Tomás Guevera lunged from the shadow of the building with a knife aimed for Rebecca's heart. His escape had gone unnoticed in the frenzy of the morning's activities. Now only inches

221

separated him from his twisted form of revenge. Of all those around her, Lone Wolf acted first.

A vicious swing of his coup stick brought the goose egg rock around in a blur. It whirred menacingly through the air before making solid contact with Tomás' temple. Fragile bone cracked and the stone buried itself to the haft. Tomás rolled up his eyes, gasped and fell dead at their feet.

Shocked, no one moved for a long moment. Then a terrible groan came from Lone Wolf's lips. Staggering like a drunken man, he approached the corpse and knelt. "I am destroyed. I am no more," he moaned.

"You saved my life, Lone Wolf," Rebecca choked out.

"And took his and wasted mine. I must return to the Black Hills at once. If there are enough days left in my husk I can redeem my black deed. Farewell, Becky. The danger has not yet abated. I am shamed until I can regain my squandered honor."

"Don't go," Rebecca begged. "I need you."

"I . . . good-bye, Becky."

After Lone Wolf's abrupt departure, the remaining prisoners were discovered cowering inside the confinement cave, although free of their bonds. Xavier led the group of victors inside his quarters.

Over bottles of wine, provided by Escobar's aides, Xavier spun out his story. Rebecca and her companions were present at Xavier's request to add their part. When it had ended, Col. Escobar rose and toasted Xavier.

"To a loyal son . . . of Mexico and of his father. You have certainly stated your case to my satisfaction. I'm authorized to grant you a full pardon, acknowledging that you were never in rebellion against Mexico, only her enemies. Well, you also proved yourself in the field, young man. I think such gallantry deserves reward. You made yourself a captain for this little campaign. I'm going to go you one better and confirm you in the rank of major."

Astonished, Xavier could not reply until he'd drained off half his glass of wine. "I'm grateful, Colonel. More than words can say. Also astonished. And a bit sad. You see, sir, I must retire from my military career to run my fath— er, my *ganadéria*. If the time ever comes the nation needs me, I will gladly and willingly serve."

The admiring, and possessive look he gave Rebecca carried a deeper meaning, one she wasn't sure she wanted responsibility for. His troubles had ended. Hers remained unresolved.

"What about Roger Styles?" she inquired.

"Forget about him. If he approaches the president, he will be taken prisoner," Col. Escobar assured her.

"Your pardon, Colonel, but I can't forget him," Rebecca answered. "As a matter of fact, I'm going after him myself. I would appreciate a platoon of Lancers for company, if possible."

"I'm afraid it can't be," Escobar informed her. "He is of no consequence."

"To me he is," Rebecca stated levelly, anger rising.

"I'll go with you," Mark McDade offered. "We came to finish him off, might as well keep at it until we do."

"Oh, Mark, thank you, thank you," Rebecca blurted. She caught herself and looked back at Xavier.

"Would nothing change your mind?" he asked weakly.

"You know better, Xavier. We've fought together and the victory is yours. Now I have to go and make sure of mine."

223

"When will you leave?" Xavier asked.

"In the morning," Rebecca answered around the tightness in her throat.

Gone were the dreams and the plans. In the end there was only Roger Styles.